D1284654

Skin Deep

Skin Deep

Sandra Diersch and Gerri London

James Lorimer & Company Ltd., Publishers
Toronto

James Lorimer & Company Ltd. acknowledges the support of the Ontario Arts Council. We acknowledge the support of the Government of Canada through the Book Publishing Industry Development Program (BPIDP) for our publishing activities. We acknowledge the support of the Canada Council for the Arts for our publishing program. We acknowledge the support of the Government of Ontario through the Ontario Media Development Corporation's Ontario Book Initiative.

Cover design: Meredith Bangay

Library and Archives Canada Cataloguing in Publication

Diersch, Sandra
     Skin deep / Sandra Diersch, Gerri London.

(SideStreets)
ISBN 978-1-55277-475-5 (bound).—ISBN 978-1-55277-474-8 (pbk.

I. London, Gerri II. Title. III. Series: SideStreets

PS8557.I385S54 2010   jC813'.54   C2009-906941-5

James Lorimer & Company Ltd.,
Publishers
317 Adelaide Street West
Suite 1002
Toronto, Ontario
M5V 1P9
www.lorimer.ca

Distributed in the U.S.by:
Orca Book Publishers
P.O. Box 468
Custer, WA USA
98240-0468

Printed and bound in Canada.

Manufactured by Webcom in Toronto, Ontario, Canada in February 2010. Job # 366649

Prologue

Corinne shut her bedroom door and leaned against it. She closed her eyes against fresh tears and hunted in the pocket of her black jacket for a tissue. Finding one that was mostly dry, she wiped her eyes then blew her nose with it. Had she ever had a worse day? All through the ceremony she'd cried. During the eulogies and the choir singing she'd buried her face in her father's shoulder and sobbed.

Sounds of movement drifted up from the kitchen. Her father's deep voice was answered by her younger brother's higher one. Back and forth in an easy rhythm they spoke to each other. A cupboard door squeaked open then banged shut. The buttons on the microwave beeped and something clattered against the countertop.

Corinne moved away from the door, hung the jacket on the back of her chair and crossed the room to the window. Outside, the May afternoon was bright — too bright. The flowers nodded their sassy heads, the birds sang. Across the street a neighbour's child played by himself on the front lawn. Corinne could see all this happening but felt as though she was looking through distorted glass, like she was watching a movie.

Was it normal to feel as disconnected from everything as she did? What was normal anyway? Nothing that had happened in the past week felt normal. Actually, nothing in the past year had been normal. The telephone rang, interrupting her thoughts. Someone downstairs answered it.

"Corinne, phone's for you," her father called.

"Tell whoever it is I'll call back later, Dad. Thanks."

Corinne kicked off her black ballet flats and slipped her feet into ratty blue slippers. She noticed a brown envelope lying on the desk. Frowning, she reached for it. It hadn't been there when she left this morning, she was sure.

She picked up the envelope and sat down on her bed to open it. Inside was a leather-bound book with the word "Journal" written in calligraphy across the front and a small slip of notepaper, folded in half. Corinne went cold at the sight of the familiar book. What was it doing in her room? Had her mother known Corinne had once peeked inside it? But that had been almost a year ago and Corinne definitely wasn't that person anymore.

With shaking fingers, she unfolded the note.

Dear Cori,

It's hard to know what to tell you, really. So many terrible things have happened this past year. I know it was hard on you, not knowing what was going on, and that you must have felt frightened and alone. I often felt that way too, and it occurred to me that perhaps it would help you to know what I was feeling through all those months of uncertainty.

So I'm leaving you my journal. I hope you will read it and learn from it. Above all, I hope you will see me in a new light when you're done, and forgive me for not always being perfectly honest with you.

I want you to know how very much I love you and how very proud I am of you. You will always be my beautiful baby girl, no matter what the future holds.

Love,
Mom

Corinne folded the note in half again and put it on the bed. She picked up the journal reluctantly and opened it to the very first paper. She ran a hand over the smooth page lovingly as she began to read. And as she read, the memories of the past year came flooding back.

Chapter 1

May 8

Was in for my yearly visit with Dr. Samuels today. She's sending me for more tests. It's just "routine," she said, but there was something in her eyes when she said it that made me wonder . . .

The crowd clustered around a picnic table in the area just off school grounds called the pit. There was a lot of laughter and good-natured jostling going on. Bright smiles gleamed in the May sun. As usual Jessica Deninsky held the others in her spell with her goddess-like beauty and perfect smile. She sat on top of the scarred green table; one long slender leg crossed over the other, cigarette held casually in her right hand, blonde hair flowing around her. Beside her was Jevon

Harding; just as perfect, just as gorgeous. Corinne could stare at him all day.

Corinne took a deep breath and let it out slowly. She reached into her pocket for the pack of cigarettes. Taking up smoking was the first step in the new image she and her best friend, Romi Singh, had planned for themselves. Smoking gave them a reason to go in the pit, where the popular kids gathered during lunch and at breaks. It would get Romi closer to Peter Sidhu — who she'd had a crush on *forever* — and Corinne closer to Jevon.

Shooting a nervous smile at her best friend, Corinne stepped through the small opening in the fence and headed to a table. As nonchalantly as she could, she handed a cigarette to Romi and took another for herself. They could do this.

Fingers trembling, she lit both cigarettes, praying Romi wouldn't choke and turn green like she had last time.

"I really don't think this is going to help," Romi whispered against Corinne's left shoulder. "Peter isn't even here."

"It's not going to work if we don't even try, Romi," Corinne hissed back.

"What do you think Jessica uses to make her hair look like that?" Corinne asked a second later. No matter how long she spent trying to tame her own dark, coarse hair and smooth out her blotchy skin, she would never look as hot as Jessica.

"How would I know?" Romi snapped.

Corinne glanced at her friend's long dark braid.

In the eight years she and Romi had been friends Romi had never had a haircut. Romi's hair always hung down her back in a smooth, thick knot.

"Should we talk to them, do you think?" Romi wondered.

Looking up, Corinne caught Jessica watching, her blue eyes perfectly made up, skin flawless. Corinne smiled at her, trying not to think of the two new zits that had popped up on her chin overnight, or her own size twelve frame. She doubted Jessica ever worried about her weight.

Jessica gave a quick nod and then tilted her head to look at the boy sitting beside her. Corinne watched helplessly as Jessica flirted with dark, muscular Jevon. He was in Corinne's English class and, like Corinne, not much of a student.

"Are you going to smoke that thing," Corinne said, glancing at the cigarette Romi held awkwardly, "or let it burn down to your fingers?" Corinne took another drag on her own cigarette. God these things tasted awful. How did anyone ever get used to it? When the smoke hit her lungs, Corinne began to cough and couldn't stop. Her eyes watered. Her throat felt like it was closing in and the smoke made her nose feel like it was on fire. Romi pounded uselessly on Corinne's back. Through the rhythmic thumps Corinne heard the titters and snorts coming from Jessica's crowd. Her face burned.

Shrugging off Romi's hand, Corinne caught the smirk on Jessica's face as she took another drag of her cigarette then blew the smoke slowly into the air.

"You okay?" Jessica called over, her voice sugary with false sympathy. "You look a little . . . green."

Her comment set the others off again. *Make a joke,* the voice in Corinne's head told her, *laugh with them.* But her tongue felt pasted to the roof of her mouth.

"What'd you do?" another voice asked. "Steal those from mommy's purse?"

Corinne straightened her shoulders and stood up. She dropped the butt and ground it out with the heel of her sneaker. "Ready, Romi?" she asked.

"Where are you going? Don't *leave* . . ." the same mocking voice pleaded as the two girls headed for the gate. Jessica and the others laughed and Corinne flinched.

"Aw, give it up you guys," a guy's voice said. Corinne's head shot up and she saw Jevon looking at her, a sympathetic smile on his face. She smiled hesitantly as she and Romi left.

They were barely through the gate before Romi had grabbed Corinne's elbow, squeezing it hard. "That was . . . the worst —" she began.

"I know," Corinne interrupted her, wrenching her arm free. "I know. I'm sorry." She tossed the pack of cigarettes into a garbage bin as they passed.

"That was so embarrassing —" Romi began again. She stopped walking so suddenly Corinne bumped into her. Looking up, Corinne saw Peter Sidhu heading straight for them.

"Hey, how's it going?" he asked as he got closer.

"Good, thanks," Romi managed to say, her eyes wide.

"It's Romi, right?"

Silently, Romi nodded. Corinne dug her elbow into her friend's side. "Yeah." Romi shot Corinne a nasty look.

"Well, see ya round, Romi," Peter said with a grin before he walked away.

Romi stared at his retreating back. Corinne giggled as she pulled her friend through the school doors. They made their way to their lockers, oblivious to the noise and confusion around them.

"I didn't know he knew my name, Cori," Romi said at last. "He must have asked someone who I was."

"That's great, Rom," Corinne said, slamming her locker shut and pulling her friend down the hall towards their next class.

"I never thought he'd notice me. I mean, we're in history together every day but he sits on the other side of the room and he's never even *looked* at me before . . ."

"I'll see you later, Rom," Corinne said as the bell rang. She gave her friend a little push into her classroom before heading down the hall to English.

When she got to her class, Corinne dropped

into a seat in the far back corner and stared at the door. Other students drifted in and took their seats. The second bell rang. Still no Jevon. She'd just seen him. Surely he wasn't going to skip?

"Get your books out, Corinne," the teacher said from the front of the room, "and get to work."

Corinne pulled her novel out of her backpack and tossed it on the desk. She was supposed to have read the first twelve chapters by today's class but she had barely gotten through six. It had to be *the* most boring book ever written.

The door opened and Jevon slipped through, dropping into his seat and flashing a guilty grin at the teacher. Corinne slowly let out a breath she hadn't even known she'd been holding.

She stared across the room at Jevon, studying the way his broad shoulders filled out his T-shirt, the way his curly black hair caught the light. He'd never even glanced at Corinne before. Why had he stuck up for them at the pit? Catching her teacher's warning glare Corinne bent her head, pretending to work. Maybe she'd been wrong. Maybe she *did* have a chance.

* * *

Romi was already at their lockers by the time Corinne got there after last period. Corinne slipped the small silver key into her lock and swung the door open. She threw her backpack in and grabbed her jacket.

"I'm absolutely *not* smoking again, Cori," Romi said.

Corinne slammed her locker door closed and jiggled the lock. "No, that's for sure. I think we need to get busy with our make-overs instead," she decided. "Why wait till summer vacation?"

They headed outside. After a cold, snowy winter it had finally warmed up in Vancouver. The trees were in full bloom; the tulips were up and Corinne could taste freedom — only five more weeks of school left. Then they could really start their transformations. New haircuts, new clothes, makeup, new looks. They'd begin grade ten right.

"Maybe this weekend?" Romi suggested.

"I have to find some money first," Corinne said as they arrived at her house. "But I'll think of something."

Waving goodbye to Romi, she let herself in. She could hear her mother's voice on the phone in the kitchen as she went upstairs to her room. Corinne dumped her books on the desk then rummaged through a pile of clothes on her bedroom floor until she found her yearbook. Flopping onto her unmade bed she opened the book and quickly found the page with Jevon's photo. *He's so perfect,* she thought, running a fingertip across the small image, *and obviously nice, nicer than his friends, anyway*. Was it possible that he could be interested in her?

Corinne slid off the bed and stood in front of her full-length mirror. She narrowed her eyes, trying to picture what she'd look like once she'd had her make-over. Shorter hair? She flicked the hem of her shirt. Definitely some new clothes. They could go to a cosmetics counter at the mall for a demonstration . . .

"Corinne, we need to talk."

Corinne spun around. Her mother stood in the doorway of her bedroom, one hand on her hip, the other holding a thin slip of white paper. Corinne's heart sank.

Her mom came in and sat on the bed. She held the slip of paper out and shook it in front of Corinne. "I'd like you to explain this note from the school. This is the *third* time I'm hearing about assignments not getting handed in or incomplete homework."

So what if it was the third note, Corinne thought. It was her problem, not her mother's. Trust her mother to blow things way out of proportion. Getting all pissed off about stuff that really didn't matter . . .

"What do you want me to say?" Corinne cried, batting the note away. "Nothing they teach you in that hole is worth anything!"

"I don't want to hear your excuses Corinne! You just can't be bothered to try. What are you doing now that we know it isn't homework? Chatting on Facebook? Listening to your iPod?" Her mom paused, watching Corinne for a reaction. Corinne gazed back at her, stubbornly silent.

Finally her mother sighed and ran a hand through her short, graying hair.

"Until you get these two assignments finished and handed in," she said at last, "and have caught up in all the other subjects you're behind in, you're grounded."

"That's not fair! God you are such a —" Her mother's steel-gray eyes stopped her.

"You'll come straight home from school each afternoon and your father or I will check your work each evening."

"I'm not a child! I don't need a homework planner like some little kid."

"Obviously, you do," her mother said, getting to her feet. She put the piece of paper on the desk and looked again at Corinne. "Read the note, Corinne. Read the part about summer school. Is that what you want? Six more weeks in a classroom while your friends are outside enjoying their holidays? And what about the rest of us? How will we fit your summer school into our plans to go away?"

Corinne said nothing, just glared at her mother until she got up and left the room, closing the door firmly behind her. Was everyone's mother this unreasonable?

Life sucks, Corinne thought, flopping onto her bed and lifting her headphones to her ears.

Chapter 2

Now comes the waiting and I'm not sure which is worse. It's nearly impossible to go about the rest of life normally with this hanging over my head. What is Dr. Samuels looking for? I'm tied up in knots of anxiety and worry. Who am I kidding? Deep down I know . . .

Corinne scowled at the layers of paper strewn across her desk and leaned back in her chair until the front legs left the floor. Since she'd basically had no choice but to do it, her school work was getting done, slowly. The fear of summer school kept her going.

She didn't really care if she failed English, or how loudly her parents nagged, but there was *no way* she was going to put up with going to summer school. Summer school would definitely screw up her plans. Not to mention how ticked Romi would be.

"How're things going?" her dad asked, pausing at her bedroom door.

Corinne grunted and let down the chair so that the legs hit the hardwood floor with a thud.

"That good, huh?"

"Did you want something?" Corinne asked, reaching for her pen. "Or are you just getting a kick out of tormenting the prisoner."

"Just tormenting the prisoner," her dad told her with a grin then moved away quickly as Corinne kicked the door shut.

She'd barely gotten back to her essay when there was a light rap on the door.

"What!" Corinne cried as her mother poked her head in the room. "I'm working, okay? Just leave me alone!"

Her mother raised her eyebrows, arms crossed. "Are you going to keep yelling at me? Or would you rather go shopping?" she asked.

Normally there was no way Corinne would go shopping with her mother, but she wasn't going to pass up an opportunity to get out of the house and spend her mom's money.

"I'm ready to leave now," her mom told her.

"Just give me a second to put on some makeup," Corinne said, standing.

"You really don't need makeup, Cori," her mother said. "Beauty is only —"

"Yeah, yeah, I've heard that one before," Corinne said. "But I'm not going out like this. Five minutes?"

Her mom rolled her eyes. "I'll meet you in the car," she called over her shoulder.

Ten minutes later Corinne climbed into the van beside her mom. She leaned her head against the headrest and looked out the window as they backed down the driveway.

It had only been a little over a week but it felt like she'd been locked in her room with her books *forever.* She found it hard to believe some kids actually *liked* studying.

"Your English teacher emailed me last night," her mother said, breaking the silence. Corinne stayed very still, waiting. "She told me how pleased she is with the change in your work habits."

"Yeah, well, it was easier than listening to you nag all the time," Corinne muttered.

"Whatever works," her mom retorted with a grin. Corinne rolled her eyes, but felt herself smiling as well.

* * *

As they pulled into the mall parking lot, Corinne wondered how much money she was going to be allowed to spend. She'd love to have a top like the one Jessica had been wearing the other day at school. It would have been more fun to shop with

Romi, Corinne thought, glancing at her mother. She wondered what the chances of ditching her mom were, now that they were here. Slim, she decided.

"Lovely Saturday madhouse," her mother muttered a few minutes later as they looked for a parking spot.

Finally they found someone just pulling out and her mother slipped into the empty space.

"Okay, you need shoes and maybe a dress for special occasions," her mother said as she and Corinne pushed through the heavy glass doors.

"I'm *not* wearing a dress," Corinne said, shuddering.

"Well, what about —" Her mom let out a shriek. "Gayle!"

A tall woman grabbed hold of Corinne's mother and pulled her into a tight hug. Heat rushed up Corinne's neck. She glanced around quickly, praying no one she knew was around.

"Melinda! I was meaning to call you this week."

"Me too. Isn't life crazy busy?"

Corinne groaned. Her mother could stand there in the middle of the mall and talk for ages, especially with one of her best friends. Corinne tuned out and turned to examine a low cut tunic-style shirt on a nearby rack. She held it up against her body, peering into the store window at her reflection. She wrinkled her nose. She didn't have a clue how women kept their boobs from falling out of these shirts. And they were expensive. Sighing, she put the shirt back.

She wondered what stores Jessica Deninsky shopped at. No matter what she wore, Jessica always looked good. Corinne would have to find some kind of job or she was never going to look as good as Jessica. Maybe she'd be a good salesperson in a clothing store. Maybe they'd give her an employee discount.

Looking up, Corinne spotted a tall, lanky boy looking at a display of running shoes. His dark blonde hair was thick and unruly and he kept pushing his glasses up on his nose. He was the kind of kid Jessica and her crowd were always making fun of. But it wouldn't take all that much to fix him up, Corinne thought, looking him up and down. Lose the glasses and the Canucks' jersey, cut that hair . . .

The boy turned suddenly and caught her looking at him. Mortified, Corinne looked down at a rack of jeans, her face burning. Would her mother ever finish yakking at Gayle?

"That's not your colour," a voice said a second later.

Looking up Corinne came face to face with glasses boy. She shrugged and walked away, ignoring him.

"You probably look best in burgundy or chocolate," he continued, following her.

Who was this loser? She tried to imagine Jevon knowing anything about clothing colours or

24

caring even. Still, how much attention did she *usually* get from guys?

"Now me on the other hand," Hockey-jersey boy went on, "I'm better in worn-out sports shirts and ripped jeans. What do you think?" He put one hand on his hip and narrowed his eyes at her in an exaggerated imitation of the male model on the poster behind him.

Despite herself, Corinne giggled. "I bet you could pull off nicer stuff if you tried," she told him, holding out a striped shirt.

The boy shrugged. "I clean up okay, if I have to," he told her. "Looks aren't everything, right?"

Corinne opened her mouth, ready to argue with him, but the arrival of her mother and Gayle stopped her.

"Oh, I see you two remember each other," Gayle said, slipping an arm around the boy. "Melinda and I were just wondering how long it had been since you'd seen each other." Gayle laughed at the confused look on Corinne's face. "This is my son, Kyle. You two used to play together quite a bit when you were younger."

"You could have said something," Corinne muttered.

Kyle grinned at her, his glasses slipping down his nose yet again. "Why? It was more fun this way, don't you think?"

"You've grown a lot, Kyle," Corinne's mom said with a smile. "I would never have recognized you."

"Tell me about it!" Gayle cried. "I can't keep

25

him in shoes. Speaking of which," she said, turning to Kyle, "we better get a move on. It was great to see you Corinne. And call me this week, Mel. Don't forget!"

Kyle linked his arm through his mom's as they walked away. They'd only gone a few steps when he looked back and winked at Corinne. She blushed.

"So, all set then?" her mother asked.

"I was ready ages ago," Corinne retorted. "You're the one who's holding us up."

"Never mind the attitude," her mom said as they walked along, peering into shops. "I haven't seen Gayle for a while; we've both been so busy. It was nice to see her looking so healthy and fit."

"Was she hugely overweight before or something?" Corinne asked. She'd already lost interest. She looked at a larger-than-life poster of a model wearing a black lace bra and panties as they passed a lingerie store. Corinne couldn't help but admire the model's figure. *Would I ever be able to look hot like that?* she wondered to herself.

"No," her mother whispered softly, following Corinne's gaze. "She had breast cancer four years ago."

Corinne could feel the heat rising to her face. She averted her eyes from the underwear model. "Sorry, I didn't know."

* * *

Two hours later Corinne dropped the bags into the

trunk of the car and slammed it shut. "I can't believe you let me buy both pairs of shoes," she said as she climbed in beside her mother. "Romi is going to be *so* green."

Her mom laughed. "Speaking of green," she said, checking over her shoulder as she backed up, "I'm going to stop at the nursery before we go home. I've been wanting to get my bedding plants."

"The nursery? Ugh, Mom. You'll be in there for . . ." Corinne suddenly remembered the pile of work waiting for her at home. Anything was better than that.

The parking lot at the nursery was packed. People were flowing out of the doors, pushing carts overflowing with bedding plants and shrubs. Corinne followed behind her mother, manoeuvering a cart carefully through the crowded aisles.

"Do you know what you want, at least?" she asked.

"Oh, I buy what speaks to me," her mother said, pausing in front of a selection of bright red flowers.

"Flowers speak to you. *Okay.*"

"Not literally, Corinne." Her mother looked at Corinne as though she were a five-year-old. "But something about a plant might appeal to me. This year I thought I might try doing something more with the corner back by that hydrangea."

"You mean that overgrown thing by Michael's

old sandbox?"

"That's a beautiful bush, Corinne. It needs a bit of pruning, that's all. I think we'll take a tray of these impatiens. They'll be perfect for the shady spots. And some of these New Guinea impatiens as well. Aren't those colours amazing?"

Corinne just rolled her eyes.

By the time her mom was satisfied, the cart was filled to overflowing and getting hard to push. Corinne glanced at her watch as they waited in line to pay.

"That wasn't so bad, was it?" her mom asked.

"We've been here over an hour."

"Really? I'm getting quicker."

"Well, you still have to put them all in the ground."

"That's the most fun, Cori. Deciding where everything should go, arranging the colours, filling the planters."

Her mother's face was so bright with excitement Corinne was almost embarrassed. They were just *flowers*. They'd be dead come October. How could anyone get so excited about something that didn't last?

Chapter 3

"MOM!" Michael screamed, the sound ripping through the quiet house.

Corinne jumped off her bed and ran to her bedroom door. She pulled it open in time to see her mother thundering down the stairs and disappearing into the kitchen.

"Good God, Michael Davies!" she heard her mother cry from the floor below. "*What* were you thinking?"

Corinne was about to close her door when the phone rang. Happy for any excuse to leave her homework, she went into her parents' bedroom and answered the phone beside the bed.

"Hello?"

"Hi Cori," her father said.

"Hey Dad," she said, perching on the edge of the carefully made bed.

"How are things? School go okay today?"

Her dad often called during the day to check in. Corinne played with the phone cord as she filled him in.

"Well, ask your mom to call me back on my cell when she can, okay?" he asked when they'd finished.

"Yeah, sure. Are you going to make it home for supper tonight?" she asked.

"I'm on my way out the door," he assured her.

Corinne put the phone back on her mother's bedside table and was turning to leave when a pamphlet caught her attention. On the front was a drawing of a nude woman, one hand cupping her breast. *Screening Mammography* was written across the top. Corinne quickly looked away, embarrassed by the image of the woman touching herself. But curiosity brought her back to it a moment later. She picked it up and opened it.

Breast self-exams, the leaflet read, *are a woman's first defense against cancer.* Corinne glanced down at the two small bumps on her own chest. Gingerly she pressed her fingertips against the fleshy side of one breast. What was she supposed to be looking for anyway?

She dropped the pamphlet on the table next to her mother's leather journal. The book was open, a pen tossed across the pages. Obviously her mother had been writing in it when Michael had screamed. Corinne wouldn't have given it another thought if her own name hadn't jumped out at her from the ivory page.

Corinne glanced at the open bedroom door then, pulse racing, she read her mother's words.

May 18

How can this have happened to me? What will I tell my daughter? Corinne needs me now more than ever, now that

A door banged and Corinne jumped, heart pumping. She heard her mother's voice and Michael answering her. They were still downstairs. Corinne took a deep breath and let it out. *Walk away Corinne,* the voice in her head told her. *This is private . . .*

But what had happened? She had to know. With trembling fingers Corinne carefully turned the page. But there was nothing else.

"You'll be fine, Michael. It's just a scratch," came her mother's voice from the foot of the stairs. Corinne jumped off the bed and fled the room through the side door to her parents' bathroom.

Safely back in her own room, Corinne closed her door and leaned against it. What was she thinking? She would kill her mother if she ever read anything private that she'd written and yet here she had done it herself. But mixed with the guilt was unease. What was her mother afraid of? What did she think had happened?

Corinne sat and tried to get back into her

homework. She couldn't stop the nervous twitch in her legs, couldn't concentrate. Was her mother sick? Going to lose her job? Question after question swirled and twisted in her head, questions that she couldn't ask.

When Corinne went downstairs to join her family for dinner, she studied her mom anxiously for clues. Going from the counter to the table with dishes of food, her mother didn't look sick, just tired. Corinne put the salad on the table and slid into her chair.

"You didn't get back to me, Melly," her dad said, helping himself to potatoes.

"I didn't know you'd called," Corinne's mom replied, sitting down finally.

Corinne felt her father's eyes burning into her. She screwed up her face and looked sheepishly from one parent to the other. "Sorry, Mom. I forgot to tell you Dad called."

Her mother raised her eyebrows at Corinne. "What if it had been important, Cori?" she asked. "You really need to be more responsible, think of the rest of us once in a while."

"I said I was sorry! God, why do you have to overreact about crap all the time!"

"I am not overreacting!" Her mother banged her glass down on the table, sloshing water over the sides. "I'm annoyed and frustrated that my fourteen-year-old daughter can't relay a simple phone message!"

Corinne stared at her mother, baffled. Like

32

Michael had never forgotten to pass on a message. Like *her mom* had never forgotten something!

"What is *wrong* with you?" Corinne cried, jumping to her feet. "God, why don't you just drop dead! Get off my back!"

The words had barely left her lips when Corinne wanted them back. She scrambled for something she could say to make things right again. But before the words came to her, her mother had left the room.

* * *

Corinne tried for over an hour to finish her final paper for English but she was too agitated, too upset by her fight with her mom. It wasn't like her mom to leave an argument like that. She was usually the one who wanted to talk everything out.

Finally Corinne abandoned her paper and wandered downstairs. Through the patio doors in the family room she could see her mother kneeling beside an empty flowerbed. Letting out a breath, she slid the door open and went out.

"Hey."

"Hey yourself," her mom said after a moment, not looking up from the tray of annuals she'd been separating.

"They're pretty," Corinne said, sitting on the bottom step of the deck.

"They are, aren't they?" Her mom pressed the soil around the little plant with firm but gentle fingers. "Get everything done then?" she asked eventually, working steadily.

"Uhh," Corinne answered. "Mostly anyway."

The musty smell of freshly turned earth hung in the evening air. Insects droned. With the addition of each plant the mound of dark soil brightened, took on life and energy.

"What's this one?" Corinne asked cautiously, kneeling beside her mom. She pointing to a taller, silvery-leafed plant her mother had placed in the centre of the others.

"Dusty Miller . . . Want to help?" her mom asked, holding out a small trowel.

"I don't have any gloves," Corinne said. Her hands were nasty enough without getting dirt caked under the nails.

Her mom pulled off her own gloves. "You can use mine," she said, handing them to Corinne. "I'll be your assistant."

Corinne pulled on the dirt-covered gloves, warm from her mother's fingers. "Does it matter what I do?" she asked.

Her mother shook her head so Corinne grabbed a plant, dug a small hole, stuck in the seedling, filled the hole, and pressed. Her mom crept backwards and sat on the step Corinne had just vacated. Out of the corner of her eye, Corinne caught her rubbing a hand across her forehead. A small streak of dirt appeared.

"Everything okay?" Corinne asked, seeing an opening.

"I'm just kind of tired today." Her mother picked at some dirt under her nails then brushed her hands on her jeans. Corinne waited but her mom stayed silent.

Corinne had just opened her mouth to say something more when she heard the gate at the side of the house creak open. Footsteps crunched on the gravel walkway. Gayle appeared from around the corner a second later. She grinned and waved.

"I can't stay," she said as she dropped down beside Corinne's mom on the step. "But I wanted to bring you these, Mel."

Gayle handed her mom a brown envelope. Corinne eyed it curiously but her mother just placed it beside her. A look passed between the two women and Corinne frowned. Gayle knew something that she didn't.

It's probably nothing, Corinne told herself, returning to the tray of flowers. *Just Mom overreacting again like she does with everything.*

Chapter 4

June 11

I'm exhausted. No sleep, just worry. Time seems to drag by as I wait for results. I spend a lot of time talking with Gayle now. She knows what I'm going through.

Corinne followed the others out of the stuffy classroom into the equally stuffy hallway. Mentally, she ticked off another day. Only five more days of classes. Two weeks after that for exams and then grade nine would be over. Corinne had crammed more effort into the past four weeks than she'd put out the rest of the year and, amazingly, she thought she just might scrape by. Of course, with her mother breathing down her neck like some kind of dragon every night it wasn't like she'd had much choice.

Other times her mom was like some kind of skittish animal; jumping at the slightest thing, preoccupied and moody. Her mind seemed miles from where her body was.

Someone rushed past, bumping Corinne's elbow. She just caught her textbook before it fell. Glaring at the girl's retreating back she adjusted her load of books.

Frowning, Corinne continued down the hallway. She rounded the corner to find Romi standing at their lockers with Peter Sidhu. He spent an awful lot of time at Romi's locker now. Was he ever going to ask Romi out? Corinne marched the last few steps down the hall.

"Hey guys, how's it going?" she asked.

"Oh, Cori! There you are," Romi said, looking up. Her eyes were bright, her cheeks flushed.

"Yup, here I am." Corinne dropped her books on the pile in the bottom of her locker and rummaged in her backpack for her lunch.

"So I'll bring you that DVD tomorrow," Peter said.

"That would be great, thanks," Romi told him. "It sounds really good."

"I think you'll like —"

"Pete, you ready to eat?" Corinne heard a voice interrupt.

Jevon. The heat rose in Corinne's neck and her pulse quickened. Plastering a smile on her face, she turned to face him. She noticed he'd had his hair cut. And he had obviously been spending a lot of time outside, judging by the tan. She longed to speak to him, but couldn't think of anything to say that wouldn't make her seem lame.

"Yeah, I'm coming," Peter said. He turned back to Romi. "I'll catch up with you later, 'kay?"

"Sure . . ."

Just as he and Peter were turning to leave, Jevon noticed Corinne standing there. "Hey, how's it going?" he asked.

"Good —" Corinne began, but they were gone. She followed Jevon's broad, muscled back as he strode down the hall and around the corner. Then she sighed and slammed her locker door shut.

Romi and Corinne took their lunches outside into the warm June afternoon. They found a tree and sat under it, faces turned to the sun.

"So?" Corinne asked when, after nearly five minutes, Romi still hadn't said anything.

"So what?"

"Has he asked you out yet?" Corinne took a big bite of her sandwich and chewed hungrily.

"No. And I don't think he's going to, really, Cori," Romi admitted. "I think he just likes me as a friend."

Corinne laughed and bits of bread flew from her lips. She covered her mouth with her hand, glancing around in case anyone caught her. Finally she swallowed and shifted so she was facing Romi.

"Peter does *not* like you as a friend, Romi, you moron," she told her. "He's probably just shy. You could always ask him, you know."

Romi's eyes widened and she shook her head vehemently. "Are you *nuts?*"

Corinne looked up at that moment to see Jessica Deninsky walk past with her crowd, even more shiny and perfect than usual. Romi followed her gaze, then looked back at Corinne and rolled her eyes. "Maybe she can ask guys out," she muttered, "but not me."

"Well, I guess you're stuck waiting till he gets up enough nerve," Corinne said with a shrug. She popped the rest of her sandwich into her mouth.

"Get off it, Cori," Romi said. "Like you'd ask Jevon out."

"I don't think Jevon even knows my name," Corinne said, tossing the sandwich wrapper into her lunch bag. She made a face at the apple she'd thrown in at her mother's insistence, and grabbed the granola bar — at least it had chocolate chips in it.

"But he did stick up for us at the pit that time," Romi reminded her. "That has to mean *something*, don't you think?"

Corinne shrugged. Surely, if it had meant something, he'd have said more than "How's it going?" when he saw her.

Though she watched for him the rest of the day, Corinne didn't see Jevon again. She walked home with Romi, only half-listening to her friend's chatter about how wonderful Peter was. It was easy for Romi to be optimistic; Peter knew her name, had sought her out. Corinne sighed. She was pretty sure Jevon was never going to ask her out. She wasn't the right shape, didn't have the right look. *But,* she reminded herself firmly, *the look is coming.*

* * *

"I'm home!" Corinne hollered as she came through the front door. She dropped her backpack on a bench and kicked off her shoes as she made her way to the kitchen.

"Mom! You home?" she called, opening the fridge.

She turned up her nose at the little containers of low-fat yogourt and the pre-cut carrots and peppers. Wasn't there anything in this house that wasn't good for you? Finally, at the back of the pantry she found a box of doughnuts. *Dad's stash,* she thought as she helped herself. *Well, hopefully he isn't keeping count.*

Voices drifted down the stairs and Corinne quickly shoved the last of the doughnut into her mouth, chewing fast. She swallowed and was licking the sugar from her fingers as her mom came into the kitchen, the phone held to her ear.

"No, that's fine, John," she said, shooting Corinne a weak smile. "Get something to eat though, will you?" her mother sighed. "Okay. Yes, I love you too. Bye." She pressed the off button and set the phone on the counter.

"Dad's going to be late tonight," she said.

"I figured. So maybe we could go out to eat then?" Corinne suggested, eyebrows raised.

"You paying?"

"I could if you raised my allowance . . ."

Her mother laughed but shook her head. "Nice try. I'll barbecue some chicken." She glanced at the clock on the microwave. "I had started to do something when your dad called. What was it?" she asked, frowning at Corinne.

"Like I know." Corinne's stomach rumbled and, reluctantly, she grabbed a yogourt from the fridge. When she turned her mother was still standing in the middle of the kitchen, staring into space. Corinne waved a hand across her mother's line of vision. "Earth to Melinda . . ."

Her mother blinked, smiled a half smile, then wandered out of the room. Corinne watched her go, a worried frown creasing her brow.

Chapter 5

June 17

I feel all black and blue. Don't want to answer any more questions. Don't want to be touched. Don't want to live like this . . .

Corinne slipped from the silent classroom and leaned against the wall, letting out a huge sigh of relief. It hadn't been as bad as she'd thought, the English final. Maybe, just *maybe* she'd pass the course. She wouldn't know for at least a week whether all her extra effort would make a difference in the end.

But right that second she was just relieved to be done. Only four more exams to go, and then she could finally start her summer. For a split second, she was grateful her parents had made her do all that extra work.

With a grin, Corinne thought of the plans she and Romi had made for that night. She was sleeping over at her friend's place and they were going to give each other facials and watch their favourite chick flicks. Glancing at her watch she wondered if Romi had finished writing her history final.

The classroom door opened beside her and Jevon slipped out. Corinne's pulse kicked up a notch or two and she cleared her throat. He shoved something in his pocket then looked up and saw her standing there. She smiled at him.

"So, how was it, do you think?" she asked, hoping her voice didn't sound as lame to him as it did to her.

Jevon shrugged. "Not bad, I guess. You do okay?"

"I hope so. Trying to avoid summer school . . ." *Now why the hell did I tell him that?*

"Been there," he said with a nod. He shifted from one foot to the other, glancing down the hallway. "Well, see ya round," he said at last and hurried away.

Corinne watched him disappear around a corner. *Well, on the one hand he stopped to talk to me. But on the other hand he didn't stay long.* She wasn't sure what to make of it all, really. Corinne's stomach growled and she glanced at her watch again. Surely Romi had finished her exam by now, she figured, and headed down the hall.

She rounded the corner by their lockers and

came to a halt, her mouth falling open in disbelief. Romi was leaning against her locker, staring up into the face of Peter Sidhu. His hand was on the wall just above Romi's head and he leaned forward as though he was about to kiss her. Corinne's heart beat faster and she ducked back around the corner. She waited a couple of seconds then peeked around again. Peter's hand was down by his side now and he'd stepped back.

Corinne stayed out of sight until Peter left. Then she ran for Romi. She didn't need to ask what he'd said. Romi's eyes shone and her skin glowed. She grabbed Corinne's hand and squeezed it tightly.

"He asked me to go to Greg Jensen's party next Saturday!" she whispered. "With him! Oh my God, Corinne! I can't believe it!"

"That's great, Romi. I told you he would ask you out eventually!" The thought breezed into Corinne's head that she had never actually *believed* he would. Maybe there was hope for Jevon and her after all.

"Oh, Corinne. I can't believe it! This is all because of you, you know."

Corinne waved the comment away. "Shut up. It's because of you. Now you're going to be part of Peter's crowd, and you won't want to hang out with me anymore . . ."

Romi looked stricken. "Why wouldn't I? You're my best friend. Oh, I *cannot* believe Peter Sidhu just asked me out on a date! But what'll I

44

wear? And what'll I say? I don't know how to talk to those guys, Corinne! Maybe you'd better come with me."

"Like Peter wants me along on your date. Can we *please* get something to eat? I'm starving. And we'll find you something to wear."

"Oh, what if my dad says no? What'll I do then? I just know he's going to ruin everything for me!"

Corinne grabbed her friend's hand and pulled her down the hall and out the doors, ignoring the steady stream of worry pouring out of Romi's mouth.

Chapter 6

June 24

It has to be a mistake. A horrible, terrible mistake. These things happen to other people, not to me. Now that I know for certain, I can't hide it from the kids anymore. What can I possibly say?

Her mother was nowhere to be found when Corinne arrived home. Corrine could hear Michael in the backyard with his best friend Torrie as she let herself into her bedroom and shut the door. For several seconds she just leaned against the door, a jaw-splitting grin on her face. She'd finished her last exam mere hours ago. No more homework, tests, lectures, essays, boring teachers, annoying classmates.

Well, for two months anyway. But right now two months sounded like tons of time. She'd left

Romi with the promise that she'd be over at the Singh house by six. In the meantime she was going to lie on her bed and do *nothing*, then she was going to have a snack and then do more nothing. In fact, Corinne decided, kicking her stuffed backpack into a corner of the room, she was going to do as much *nothing* as she could cram into each and every day.

She lay on the bed and tucked her hands behind her head. It was warm in her room with the mid-afternoon sun streaming through the window. Corinne's eyes grew heavy. Suddenly her pocket started vibrating. She pulled out her cell and saw on call display that it was Romi.

"What now?" she said into the phone.

"Bring some snacks, 'kay?" her friend told her. "And have you got any good colours of nail polish?"

Corinne frowned, mentally going through her dresser. "Not really. But I could stop and pick some up if you want."

"Naw, don't bother," Romi told her. "I've got enough. Hey, if you were going to stop, though, you could pick up some of those toe separator thingies."

"Yeah, okay. I'll get some. I'll see you at six."

"What were you doing?" Romi asked.

"Lying on my bed doing absolutely nothing," Corinne told her. "And if you'd stop calling me I could get on with it."

She turned her phone off and tossed it on her

bedside table. Corinne wriggled around on the duvet until she found a comfortable sleeping position.

* * *

"Bye! I'm going over to Romi's now," Corinne called, heading for the back door later that evening. She'd spent the last part of the afternoon shredding all her school notes, every assignment and test from all her classes. And it had felt *good*.

"Hold on a second, Corinne." Corinne's mother came into the kitchen just as she was slipping her feet into her flip-flops. Corinne looked up as she swung her bag over her shoulder. "I'll be home by noon tomorrow," she began, then paused. Her mom looked positively *gray*.

"Your father and I need to talk to you and Michael," her mom said, her voice tight.

Now? When I'm about to start my summer? For a second Corinne considered just heading out the door. Finally she dropped her bag to the floor and followed her mother into the living room, where her father was already sitting with Michael.

Michael was frowning at the little screen of his computer game. The blips and thunks of the game were the only sound in the room. Her mother sat on the sofa and motioned for Corinne to sit down.

"Michael, put the game down. Turn it off and put it on the table," their father said.

"I just want to finish this level . . ." Michael

48

said, eyes never leaving the game.

Their dad didn't speak as he reached out and snatched the game from his son, dropping it in his lap.

"I need you to listen very carefully to what I'm going to tell you," their mom began. Her voice was suddenly raspy and soft.

Their dad reached over and took her hand, holding it between his own, as if giving her the energy to keep going with what she had to say. Corinne stared at their clenched hands and she knew even as her mother said the words that this was going to change their lives. She had never seen her parents so serious before. Suddenly, Corinne was more scared than she had ever been in her life.

"I don't know how else to tell you this, so I'm just going to come out and say it." Their mother paused and took a deep breath. "I have breast cancer," she blurted. Her voice broke slightly at the end.

Corinne sat staring at her mother as the words sunk in. When her mom tried to make eye contact with her, Corinne looked away, at the photograph hanging on the wall just behind her left shoulder, anywhere other than her mother's eyes. Corinne's hands began to shake and she shoved them under her legs as her mother's voice rushed in to fill the silence.

"I'll be going into the hospital for surgery in a few weeks," she said. Her words started coming out faster and faster, as if anything she said now could possibly help with what they were all feeling. "I may have to have chemotherapy and radiation treatments afterwards to help make sure it's all gone."

"We're going to have to be strong together, guys," their father cut in. "Help each other out."

Corinne looked at him. He was still holding his wife's hand. His skin had a grayish colour to it too, just like her mom's did. There were dark circles under his eyes. He looked *old*. Then it dawned on Corinne that her parents must have known what was going on for weeks already. Corinne thought back to the diary entry she had read. *How could this have happened* . . . but that was over a month ago.

"Yes, that will be important. After I come out of the hospital I'll need a lot of rest —"

"Does it hurt?" Michael interrupted.

"Moron," Corinne muttered under her breath.

"No, sweetheart," their mom told him. "Nothing hurts."

"Then how do you know there's anything wrong?" he demanded.

Corinne looked from person to person as the other members of her family spoke. She could see their lips moving, but she could no longer *hear* the words over the roaring in her ears. Corinne shivered. She felt so cold, and she couldn't stop the trembling in her hands. She hugged herself, confused by her reaction. She had *known*. She

50

began to put the pieces together: the pamphlet on the bed, the journal, the envelope from Gayle, her mom's strange behaviour lately. How could she be so surprised now? *Because I didn't want to believe anything could really be wrong with my mom.*

"And what about our holidays?" Michael cried, startling Corinne out of her thoughts. "You *promised* we'd go to Drumheller this year!"

"Michael," his father cautioned.

"We did say we'd go to Drumheller this summer, Michael," his mom told him gently. "And I'm sorry we have to change our plans . . ."

Michael's face turned scarlet and his fingers balled up into fists. He jumped up off the couch. "You're not sorry at all! You probably never wanted to go to the dinosaur museum anyway!"

He ran from the room. A second later a door upstairs slammed shut, making the windows rattle.

"You want me to go after him?" Corinne's dad asked, starting to stand.

Her mom put a hand on his arm, pulling him down again. "No, leave him, John. Give him some time alone."

Two fat tears broke free and rolled down Corinne's cheeks.

"Corinne?" Her mother came and knelt at Corinne's feet. "Cori?" she asked, stroking Corinne's hair then cupping her cheek with her hand.

"I didn't mean to dump it on you, Cori," she murmured. "We wanted to wait until school was

51

finished. There wasn't any good way to say it."

"No," Corinne agreed, wiping at her cheeks.

"Are you okay?" Her mom's voice was soft, a caress. And her hand was warm. Corinne leaned into it.

"I'm okay," she lied.

"Do you have any questions? Anything you want to know?"

"When's the surgery?" Corinne asked.

"July fifteenth. Three weeks."

Corinne nodded.

"Gayle said to tell you that if you ever want to talk but don't want to talk to me, she's a phone call away," her mom told her. "Okay? Will you promise me you'll ask your questions? Talk if you need to? Don't keep it all locked inside?"

"Yeah, sure. Do you mind if I go to my room?" she asked, avoiding her mother's anxious eyes as she stood up. "I think I just need to be by myself for a bit."

"Of course. Sweetie, everything will be . . ." Her mother's voice trailed off as Corinne went upstairs.

She had just shut the door when her cell started buzzing at her. Corinne cringed.

Romi.

"Where are you Cori? Are you coming?"

Corinne swallowed hard and let out a breath. "I'm sorry Romi," she began, clearing her throat. "Something's come up and I can't come over tonight."

There was silence at the other end. Corinne shut her eyes as she waited. "Is everything okay?" Romi asked at last.

"Yes. No —" Corinne stopped, took a second then began again. "Can I come over to your place tomorrow morning?"

"Well, sure, but —"

"Thanks, Romi. Sorry about tonight," Corinne murmured, snapping the phone shut.

She sat on the edge of the bed and stared at her hands in her lap, watching each tear drop onto her skin.

Chapter 7

June 25

I hate that I'm putting my family through this. It's getting so hard to pretend that we'll all be okay — that I'll be okay.

Romi was waiting at the door when Corinne got to her house Thursday morning. Romi's place was a large, sprawling two-storey house on a big lot with tons of trees. Inside it was chaotic and comfortable. It wasn't very often Romi's home was empty. With two older brothers and one younger, her parents and her grandmother, the Singh house was always busy. This morning, however, the house was strangely quiet.

"Where is everyone?" Corinne asked as she followed Romi upstairs to her room.

"Oh, work, appointments, you know. Great,

isn't it?" Romi grinned, then her smile faded as she looked at Corinne. "What's going on Cori? Is everything okay?"

"My mom has breast cancer."

Romi covered her mouth with her hand. "Oh Corinne, no! My God! Is she, will she . . ."

"She goes for surgery in a few weeks."

"Are you okay? How's your mom?"

Romi's dark eyes were glassy with tears and Corinne felt her own eyes sting and burn. She swallowed hard and shook her head.

"I'm kind of freaking out, I guess. But Mom's pretty positive."

"Well, that's good."

"But Romi, what if she doesn't make it? What if it doesn't matter how positive her attitude is? Then what?" The knot that had grown in Corinne's stomach since her mother's announcement started to burn. Romi reached for her hand and squeezed it. She led Corinne to her bed and sat down beside her, keeping hold of her hand.

"Try not to think the worst, Cori. Lots of people survive cancer, lots more than ten years ago."

"And lots don't."

"Well hopefully they caught it real early and the surgery takes care of it," Romi said, a little too brightly.

"What if it isn't early enough?" Corinne whispered, tears filling her eyes.

"Isn't it better to be positive?"

Romi was trying, Corinne knew she was, but it

was all suddenly too much.

"But what if it *isn't?*" She collapsed against her friend and cried while Romi held her.

Finally the tears subsided and Corinne pulled away. She blew her nose and wiped her face and then sat, staring at the soggy tissue in her hand.

"Sorry," she said softly.

"You don't have to apologize to me," Romi said with a wave of her hand. "I wish there was something I could do to help."

"You have, Rom," Corinne assured her. She blew her nose again, threw the used tissues in the wastebasket and cleared her throat.

"I know! Let's get your mind off it for a while. Why don't we think about what I'm going to wear on my date with Pete tonight instead?"

* * *

Corinne lay in bed later that night, the silence of the house pulsing around her. Now and then she could hear bedsprings squeak as her brother rolled over in his sleep. He was still so angry, banging things around, snapping at everyone, but especially at their mom, complaining about his lost holiday.

Her parents had come upstairs a while ago, speaking softly to one another. Likely her dad had been touching her mother, holding her hand or an elbow, a shoulder, *something*. It was as though he was afraid that if he didn't keep a hand on her, she

56

could disappear. Corinne felt the tears springing up again, but she choked them back.

"Enough already," she muttered, swinging her legs out of bed. She couldn't lie there any longer and pretend she would be able to sleep.

She slid open the patio door and stepped out onto the deck; the cedar boards were still warm under her feet. She lay down on a lounger and tucked her hands behind her head. With the outdoor lights on around the yard it wasn't completely dark, but she could still see the stars and the yellow crescent of moon hanging in the sky. A breeze blew and brought the scent of flowers with it.

Beneath an ornamental cherry tree sat several trays of annuals, still in their little plastic pots. Other than that one bed Corinne and her mom had planted nearly a month ago, nothing had been done. The planters sat empty on the deck; the beds along the fence were bare.

Corinne took a deep breath and let it out slowly. Shakily she sat up and swung her bare feet to the deck. Gripped with fear, and desperate for any way of making things better, Corinne got up from the lounger. She found the gloves and a spade and knelt in front of a mound of dirt.

* * *

Corinne climbed the wooden steps back to the deck and lay down on the lounger. Flowers filled the beds around the yard, the planters on the deck, and even cascaded from hanging baskets hung around the shed. It had taken Corinne half the night to plant everything her mother had bought in the semi-darkness.

Corinne heard a bump and a scrape by the house and looked over to see Michael stepping outside in his bare feet. He barely looked at his sister as he sat down, his tattered old sock animal in his arms.

For a long time she and Michael sat silently watching the sky. An owl flew lazily by, its huge wings making a swish-swishing in the silence. Somewhere a car alarm went off and blasted its warning for several minutes before stopping.

"Is Mom going to die?"

Corinne jumped, her elbow banging the edge of the lounger. For a second she had forgotten Michael was outside with her. She stared at the house, rubbing her throbbing elbow.

"Is she, Cori? Is she going to die?"

"No."

"But how do you know? Torrie's grandmother had cancer and she died."

"Torrie's grandmother was an old woman."

"Eddie's brother died of cancer two years ago and he was only thirteen. Eddie said they couldn't find a donor for him and he died. Will they find a donor for Mom? Could I be one?"

Corinne felt the sting of tears behind her eyes and her heart ached with every beat. "Mom doesn't have that kind of cancer, Michael," she said, her voice rough. "She has breast cancer. They don't use donors for that. They just do the surgery and the treatments and hope she'll be okay."

There was a shuffle and a pebble rattled across the cedar as Michael left his chair to climb onto hers. Corinne slipped an arm around his thin shoulders and he leaned against her, his stuffed creature tickling her nose.

"Cori?"

"Yes, Michael."

"Do you think I'm a baby because I started sleeping with Foxy again?"

"No."

"Corinne?"

"Yes?"

"I'm scared."

"Me too."

Chapter 8

July 6

What have I done to deserve this? What has my family done? I did everything they say you should do and in the end it didn't matter! I only ever wanted to live well, to be a good example to my kids. And now. Now my children wander around the house stunned and terrified. And it's my fault. All of it . . .

Corinne stared out the window watching the raindrops hit the glass, bead, and roll down. The weather mirrored exactly how she felt heading for her first day of summer school. Four lousy percentage points! Four! Corinne rolled her eyes. She still couldn't quite believe she'd missed a pass by four percent. There really was no justice in the world.

The traffic report droned on the radio and her dad drummed his fingertips on the steering wheel as they idled at an intersection.

"Got everything you need?" he asked as they began to move again.

"Yeah, I'm fine."

"You're okay coming home on the bus?"

"I said I'm fine."

"Just checking, Cori, you don't need to snap at me," her father said, hurt.

Corinne turned around with a small sigh. "Sorry. I'll be okay."

"I had to take summer school one year — did I tell you that?" Her dad turned the radio down and cleared his throat. Corinne closed her eyes to block out his fidgeting. He never used to be a fidgety person.

"No, you never did."

"It was grade eleven. Failed geography. I don't use geography a heck of a lot in my job, that's for sure," he said with a laugh.

"Not like English, huh?" Corinne commented dryly. Would they ever get there?

"Just do your best, Cori, that's all we ask."

Corinne turned back to her window. The knots in her stomach were growing tighter the closer they got and her mouth had gone dry. There was so much stuff in her head already, how would she ever find room for grammar and novels? How could her dad get his brain wrapped around writing estimates for print jobs when Mom's surgery got closer and closer every day? When they didn't know what the rest of the summer held? Or the rest of their lives?

"Dad, are you afraid?" she blurted as the school loomed suddenly in front of them.

He didn't answer right away. Finally Corinne turned to look at him. He was staring at the road, his hands white-knuckled on the steering wheel. "It's important to stay positive, Cori," her dad said at last.

He checked over his shoulder, changed lanes and slid to a stop against the curb in front of the two-storey brick building.

"That's not what I asked."

"Your mother is going to be just fine. She's got good doctors, a great surgeon. They've caught the growth early. Don't you worry about anything, okay? Just go and do your best today."

Admitting defeat, Corinne gave her father a quick peck on the cheek and climbed out of the car. She swung her backpack over her shoulder, rain quickly soaking her clothes, and watched as he drove away.

Finally she walked up the path to the front doors. Inside lists of classes and room numbers were posted along the corridor by the office. She found hers and then checked the large map. Her own high school was small and very new compared to this dungeon, she realized as she climbed the stairs.

There were about twenty-five other kids

already in the room when Corinne found her class. She slid into a seat near the window. She would have preferred not to sit right at the front of the class, but at least by the window she could look at something other than her fellow rejects.

She pulled out her notebook and a pen and sat picking at her nails, waiting for the teacher. She was working on her right hand when she felt a light tap on her shoulder. The girl sitting behind her grinned and snapped her gum. Her long dark hair was streaked with white-blonde highlights, giving her a zebra-like look.

"Do you have a pencil or pen I could borrow?" she asked. "My little shit of a sister must have raided my bag before I left."

"Yeah, sure. Hold on." Corinne found her spare pen and handed it to the girl.

"Thanks a ton. You're a lifesaver. I'm Bree, by the way. Short for Breanna."

"Corinne."

"So, what'd you fail by?"

"What?" Corinne pulled her eyes away from Bree's amazing hair and frowned. There was something vaguely familiar about Breanna but Corinne couldn't think what it was.

"I failed by five percent," Bree said. "Last year it was three. I complained but they just told me some stupid-ass story about having to draw the line somewhere."

"Four," Corinne told her. "I thought about complaining but I didn't get around to it."

"Well, don't bother. You know, you look real familiar to me. What school do you go to?" Bree asked, frowning at Corinne.

Corinne told her and a wide smile spread across Bree's face. "I thought so! You were in my algebra class last year. Remember?"

"Algebra?" Corinne had spent most of that class in a fog of confusion. But then a vague memory came to her. "Oh yeah! You sat at the far side of the room and used to ask tons of questions."

"And you spent the whole hour with your head on your desk or staring out the window," Bree said with a shriek of laughter. "You probably didn't recognize me 'cause I'm so drop-dead gorgeous now. Probably get invited to all the popular parties this year. As if I'd go. Bitches and jerks, all of them."

Corinne lowered her head to hide the sudden flush of pink in her cheeks. What did Bree know about those people, anyway? She was probably just jealous because she wasn't a part of the group. When she looked up again, Bree had gathered her bizarre mass of hair together in one hand and was quickly braiding it.

"Cool colour, huh?" she asked, catching Corinne's stare. "Did it myself."

"It's very different," Corinne said cautiously.

Bree laughed. "It looks hideous, liar," she said cheerfully. "But I was tired of plain old dark brown. Sorry, no offense," she said quickly as

64

Corinne unconsciously touched her own hair.

"Don't worry about it. I hate my hair too but I don't have the guts to colour it myself and I'm broke."

"Well, if you want *me* to do it . . ." Bree offered with a cheeky grin as the bell rang.

Bree's muttered one-liners and the fact the teacher was both young and, surprisingly, kind of interesting, helped Corinne make it through her first day of summer school.

When the bell rang at noon she and Bree walked out together, their backpacks crammed with homework.

"Can you believe she wants us to have the first *twelve* chapters read by tomorrow?" Bree complained as they made their way outside into the hot summer afternoon. "I didn't read twelve chapters all of last year."

"Guess that's kind of why we're here, huh?" Corinne said.

"Whose side are you on?" Bree demanded.

"I'm just saying . . ."

They reached the sidewalk and Bree waved at a woman waiting in a car. "There's my mom," she said. "See you tomorrow."

"See ya, Bree."

Corinne arrived home half an hour later, hot, hungry, and tired. She dumped her pack at the front door, kicked off her flip-flops and headed for the kitchen. Through the screen door she could see her mother and brother at the picnic table. Her mom looked up and waved.

"Hey, Cori, come out and have some lunch with us," she called. "I left you a sandwich in the fridge."

"So, how was it?" her mother asked after Corinne joined them.

"It was okay," Corinne told her with a shrug. "The teacher's kind of interesting. We have a ton of homework, though — twelve chapters for tomorrow and some grammar exercises."

"What kind of exercises?" Michael asked. "Push-ups? Sit-ups?" He got up from the table, laughing loudly at his joke. Corinne rolled her eyes.

"You need a new writer," she muttered as he disappeared into the house.

Her mom smiled. "It sounds like a lot, but I've seen you polish off an entire novel in a day when you want to."

"Well, sure, when it's a book *I've* picked out," Corinne said.

Her mom laughed and took a sip of her tea. "Lordy it's hot out here, isn't it? Would you look at those poor flowers?"

"I'll water them when the sun is off the yard," Corinne said. "Don't want them to burn."

"You did a great job with them, by the way. But I always like to water first thing in the morning," her mother told her. "It's so peaceful and quiet out here and the heat hasn't hit yet."

"Well, I'm not getting up any earlier than I

already do just to water the garden!" Corinne snapped. She was still a little upset that it had taken days before anyone noticed that she'd planted flowers, even.

"No one said you had to!" her mother snapped back.

They glowered at each other until a sparrow scolded them from the cherry tree, breaking the tension. Tiny pangs of guilt hit Corinne like pinpricks. She cleared her throat and looked up at her mom sheepishly.

"So, uhm, I was thinking of moving some of those impatiens from the bed by the hydrangea," Corinne said. "That spot beside the shed looks a little bare."

"There's an extra planter around here some-where," her mom said. "We could put them in that, add some height. I'll go get it."

Chapter 9

July 10

I stood before the mirror, naked, just looking at my breasts. In less than 24 hours they will be gone. Will I still be a woman without them? And John, how will I let him see me naked? How could anyone find a flat-chested, scarred middle-aged woman desirable?

"You have to come with us, Corinne! I want you there. It'll be *fun*." Romi rolled over onto her back and stretched. Corinne and Romi had been sprawled on towels in Corinne's sunny backyard all afternoon. The sun on their bare skin felt good.

"Are you sure I'm invited?" Corinne ached to go, but this was Jessica's crowd.

"It's not like that," Romi explained. "A bunch of us are going and I want you to come. Don't you want a break from summer school and, you know, *stuff?*"

"Well yeah, but . . ."

"*He's* going to be there, Cori," Romi said slyly. "And, a certain blonde *won't* be."

"Romi, just because you snagged Peter doesn't mean we're all going to suddenly have boy-friends."

Romi laughed easily and quickly these days and seemed to float over the ground without actually touching it. She mentioned Peter every second sentence and she'd stop talking all of a sudden and smile a funny smile, staring off into space. She seemed to spend almost all of her time with Peter. Not that Corinne had much free time between summer school, homework, and dealing with stuff at home.

But an entire afternoon with Jevon . . . When would Corinne ever have the chance to spend this much time with him? And without Jessica for competition? She felt herself nodding.

"Awesome! Hey, we have a few days, let's get to the spa and get some work done. What do you think?"

"I'm broke, remember?" Corinne said. "And Mom refuses to loan me any more money until I pay off what I owe. Which'll probably be when I retire."

"No problem! Mom and Dad gave me a gift certificate to a spa — a present for making honour roll again. I'll share it with you."

"You don't want to share it with me."

Romi stood up and adjusted her bikini bottom. "I offered to share it. Do you want to go or not?"

"Sorry. Yeah, let's make an appointment."

Romi brightened. "Good. Okay. Well, I better get going. Peter's picking me up at six. Call me tomorrow, okay?"

Corinne watched her friend as she pulled her sundress on overtop of her suit. She had spent the last couple of hours trying to even out her tan so that her strap lines wouldn't show. When Romi had finally disappeared around the corner, Corinne went in search of her mother. She found her propped against the headboard of her bed, a blanket over her feet.

"Romi gone?" her mom asked as Corinne entered the room.

"Yeah, just now. Were you sleeping?" Corinne asked, perching on the edge of the bed.

"Maybe a bit. What's up?" her mom asked.

"Romi's invited me to a beach party. Can I go?" she asked hopefully.

"Yes, you can go," her mother told her with a smile. "When is it?"

"Next Wednesday, the fifteenth."

The smile left her mom's face. She pushed herself up in the bed. "The fifteenth? That's the day I go into the hospital, Corinne."

Corinne's heart beat more quickly. Still, she spoke calmly.

"But you don't go in until that night, for tests

and stuff?" she said. "Your surgery isn't actually until the next morning."

"I don't know . . ." A deep frown creased her mom's forehead.

Suddenly the party became the most important thing in Corrine's summer. So far it had been nothing but school and worry.

"I'll go from school to the beach and I'll be home before dinner," she said, struggling to remain calm. There was *no way* she was missing out on this chance to have some fun.

"Maybe another day would be better," her mother said.

"You just said I could go!" Corinne cried, jumping to her feet. "I'll be home before you leave for the hospital!"

"Stop yelling at me!"

Corinne crossed her arms over her chest. "Well, it's not fair! What am I supposed to do around here all afternoon? Hold your hand?"

"Corinne!" Her mother's face was red, her eyes wide and shining with sudden tears.

The guilt prickles began to form again in Corinne. This time they ran up and down her spine. But she held on to her anger and sense of injustice. "Well, what is it that you want from me? Don't I get any summer at all? I promised to be home in time to go with you to the hospital."

Her mother opened her mouth, then shut it again. She took several deep breaths. Corinne's own breathing was coming hard and fast as well.

71

She didn't care what her mother said next, she was going to the beach with Romi next Wednesday.

"Fine, go. Have fun." Her mother slid down in the bed and rolled over.

"Fine, I will," Corinne muttered and went to phone Romi.

* * *

Corinne smoothed out the edges of her cherry red towel and adjusted her water bottle slightly. She leaned back against the large log and stretched her legs out in front of her. Beside her Peter and Romi were giggling as they arranged their blanket, taking every opportunity to touch each other on the hand, the arm, the leg.

Spread out in front of them the waters of English Bay lapped the shore gently. A few people splashed in the water and some children played at the edge with their buckets and shovels. Beyond them boats bobbed in the waves and a sailboat strayed, barely moving in the calm.

From two blankets down came the familiar deep chuckle of Jevon's laugh. Corinne's pulse quickened and she closed her eyes behind her sunglasses. In the hour that they'd all been together, all Jevon had said to Corinne was, "Hey, how's it going?" In fact, except for Romi, that was all anyone had said to Corinne since she had joined the group at the bus stop.

She shifted in the sand, trying to find a

comfortable position to sit. The bikini wax she'd had done the day before was still irritated, although the redness was fading, thankfully. Corinne winced just remembering the pain of hair being ripped by the roots from her body. How did people do that all the time?

Loud shouts of laughter drifted over the sand and Corinne turned to see Jevon and two other guys wrestling. The girls squealed as sand flew up and there were more shouts and laughter.

She started to say something to Romi, but turned away again quickly, her face flaming, when she saw that her friend was tangled up with Peter on the blanket. Seeing her best friend making out with her new boyfriend just made Corinne feel even more lonely. Somehow, in the past two weeks, Romi had become a popular girl too. Corinne had noticed it at the bus stop.

Romi had an ease and confidence she'd never had before. She wore a bright purple sarong over her white bikini and her black hair swung perkily in its ponytail. Nothing about Romi had been perky before. Had dating Peter really made that big of a difference?

A baseball cap flew through the air and landed on the sand next to Corinne's blanket. She looked up, shielding her eyes with her hand. Jevon was standing in the sand several feet away, laughing as he scanned the beach for his cap.

Corinne took a deep breath and stood up. She grabbed the ball cap and walked slowly over, trying not to feel self-conscious wearing only a bikini. None of the other girls were concerned about body parts falling out or looking fat.

"Did you lose this?" Corinne asked, smiling as she held out the cap.

Jevon reached out and took it from her. "Oh, thanks."

"No problem," Corinne said, struggling to keep her hands at her sides and not crossed over her chest. "It's real hot today, eh?"

"Yeah."

"Are you having a good summer so far?" she continued, a little surprised by her bravery.

"It's okay. I'm working for my dad and stuff," Jevon said with a shrug. He leaned down and pulled a pack of cigarettes out of his bag. He tapped one into his hand then offered the pack to Corinne.

Corinne reached for it, and then let her hand drop as her mother's face popped into her head. "No thanks," she said quietly, her ears hot.

"Whatever." Jevon lit his own cigarette and took several quick puffs and then he lowered himself to his towel and leaned back against the log. "Thanks for bringing my hat back, Connie."

"It's Cori . . ." she corrected him, but her voice trailed away as a slender shadow fell across the towel.

"Jess!" Jevon cried, jumping up. "What're you doing here? Aren't you supposed to be in Calgary till Saturday?"

74

Jessica Deninsky's tinkling laugh drifted over Corinne as she stood awkwardly beside Jevon's towel. Slowly she started to inch away, her eyes focused on her painted toenails.

What had possessed her to do that? Just 'cause the guy had stuck up for them that day in the pit, had said a couple of nice words to her in the hall didn't change anything. She sat down on her towel and pulled a T-shirt over her bikini.

Eyes burning, she grabbed her bag, hiding her face as she rummaged through it. She pushed aside the plastic container of sunscreen her mom had added and finally found her novel for English class. Opening it, she began to read.

"Come swimming with us, Cori?" Romi asked, surfacing at last from her make-out session.

Corinne looked up, shielding her eyes with her hand. Her friend's mouth was red and sore-looking, her hair flying loose from its ponytail. "Maybe later," she said, and turned back to her book.

Romi crouched down, her head tilted. "What's wrong? Aren't you having fun?"

Corinne tried hard not to laugh in her friend's face. "I just have this reading to do," she lied. "You go ahead swimming. Peter's waiting for you."

"You don't have to do that right this second, Cori! God, we're on the beach! We're going to have piggyback fights in the water."

And who exactly would be my partner? Corinne

wondered, but didn't bother to ask. What was the point?

"Romi, are you coming or what?" Peter called.

Romi stood up slowly, still looking at Corinne, but Corinne gave her a quick smile and went back to her book. When Romi finally ran down the beach and joined the others, Corinne looked up again.

There was a lot of squealing and laughing as girls climbed onto boys' shoulders, more screaming and splashing as they were knocked off. Shiny, perfect hair whipped in the sunlight, tanned arms and legs glistened with water, and tinkling laughter filled the summer air. The boys all looked like movie fighter pilots with their mirrored sunglasses and muscled bodies. Jevon, especially, had the look of a god, which seemed only fitting considering who was perched on his shoulders.

Even at the beach, Jessica Deninsky looked perfect. She wore a designer tankini; her skin was a perfect shade of copper, her blonde hair shiny and bouncy. She looked smug sitting up there, like she'd won a contest.

Corinne should never have come. She was only there because Romi had asked her. The others didn't know she was alive. It wouldn't matter how much time she spent at the spa and hair salon or how trendy her clothes were, she wasn't a part of this group and never would be.

Chapter 10

July 15

I can't believe that Corinne abandoned me. Today,
of all days. Doesn't she know how frightened I am?
The surgery, not knowing. What if they don't get
all the cancer? What if there are complications?
What if I die?

Later
It's better she's with her friends, enjoying the day.
I can let her have this.

Corinne sat huddled in a chair and stared out the
window. It was horrible. They were all crowded in
the hospital room, her dad, Corinne, Michael, and
her mother on the bed. The window was closed
and, although there was air conditioning, the air
was thick and close from too many bodies, too

much emotion. She could smell the fear seeping from their pores.

Her father kept fussing, pulling at his wife's blanket, refilling her water glass, adjusting the pillow behind her. "Are you warm enough, Melly?" he asked for the third time. "Should I get you some juice or ice chips? Should I open the window?"

"John, love, I'm fine."

He nodded but in no time he was fussing again. Corinne wanted to slap at his hands and scream at him to sit still. She wished she were anywhere but where she was. Her brother climbed onto the bed beside their mother.

"Mom?"

"Yes, Michael."

"Do you think that when they go to do your operation, that the . . . the cancer could just be gone?"

"That's not going to happen, Michael, you moron. Cancer doesn't just disappear," Corinne said from her chair by the window. It was one thing to be innocent, but didn't the kid get *any* of it?

"No, unfortunately it doesn't just disappear. But the doctors can take it away and that will help make me better."

"You don't look sick. How do they know there is really anything wrong? Maybe they made a mistake with the pictures. Maybe those pictures are someone else's."

Corinne felt herself listening carefully, hopeful,

despite herself. Couldn't they have made a mistake? Were they absolutely sure it was her mother's X-ray that showed cancer?

"They are very, very careful about the pictures, Michael. They don't make mistakes like that. But the operation I am having tomorrow is going to get rid of the cancer and then I'll be much better. Remember? I told you about that."

Then she'll be much better, Corinne repeated in her head.

* * *

Later that evening Corinne left her mother's room in search of something to eat. There was a vending machine near a small common room. She stood before it, studying her choices. *Even in a hospital you can find junk food,* she thought. She bought a chocolate bar, and ate it as she headed back down the hall. She'd sit with her mom until visiting hours were over, then catch the bus home.

Corinne had felt her father's reluctance to leave more than an hour ago. "You're sure you don't want me to stay the night?" he had asked, taking her mother's hand.

"No," Corinne's mom had told him, her voice firm. "Michael needs to be at home. I'll see you first thing. I'll be fine."

"I'll stay for a while," Corinne had said. She hadn't wanted to leave her mother then either. "I'll take the bus home later. It's okay, Dad."

79

But after her father and brother had left, Corinne wasn't sure staying had been such a good idea. Everything, every sentence, every brave smile felt forced and awkward. She had thought she might fall apart completely if she had to stay another second in that hospital room, so she'd made an excuse to get out of there for a moment.

Now, as she pushed open the door to her mom's room, she saw that the curtain was pulled across the bed, blocking it from view. Fear swept through her. What were they doing to her? Why had Corinne left her alone? As she put her hand out to move the cloth aside she heard her mother's voice. It was low and urgent.

"Promise me, Gayle, that you'll help John with the kids if I die. Corinne will need a woman to turn to."

Corinne's hand flew to her mouth and she choked back a sob. She couldn't move: her brain seemed unable to send the right messages to her legs.

"You know I would, but there isn't going to be any need for that."

"How do you know? We're just fooling ourselves, saying words we think the other one wants to hear. Please don't act a part with me, Gayle. I have to act with John and the kids. Please, not with you, too."

"I *know* how frightened you are and I know how hard it is to be positive. I *understand*, Melly, I do!"

There was a creak of bedsprings and a muffled sob.

"I want to believe you," Corinne heard her

mom say a moment later, "but right now it seems too much to hope for."

"It is not too much to hope for, Melly."

Corinne swallowed hard and backed out of the room silently. In the corridor she slid down the wall until she was sitting on the floor. What was her mother doing here in this cold, sterile place? These things happened to other people. Not *her* mom. Her eyes burned and her throat tightened.

Suddenly a hand squeezed her shoulder. Corinne looked up, startled. "Kyle?" she said as he dropped to the cold floor beside her.

"How're you doing, Cori?" he asked.

The question, the kindness in his voice, his presence beside her, wiped away the last little bits of Corinne's self-control. She put her head down on her knees and sobbed.

Eventually her sobs subsided and Corinne became aware of Kyle's arm around her shoulder. Cheeks burning, she pulled away and struggled to her feet.

"I'd better go in, my mom will be wondering where I went," she said, her voice rough. Kyle grabbed her hand.

"You don't need to hide your tears from me, Corinne," he told her gently. "But don't let your mom see them."

Nodding, Corinne tilted her head back until she could see the discoloured ceiling tiles. She blinked fiercely and took several deep breaths, all the while hanging on tightly to Kyle's hand.

"Will you wait?" she asked when, at last, she felt more in control.

"Yeah, I'll be here," he assured her, pointing down the hall to a bench.

Corinne sniffed and nodded her head. As she pushed the door open it crossed her mind that she hadn't asked why Kyle had come. But in the second before she went around the curtain to where her mother waited, she realized she really didn't care *why* he was there, only that he was.

* * *

Gayle had given Kyle money for a taxi to take them both home. Corinne had planned to take the bus — it wasn't far — but as they settled into the cracked leather of the cab's backseat, she was glad of the privacy. Her emotions were all so close to the surface she was sure they'd spill over at any second. She held tightly to Kyle's hand where it lay on the seat between them but neither of them said a word until the taxi pulled into Corinne's driveway.

"I know it's hard, Cori," Kyle said as she unbuckled her seatbelt. "But try to hang on, okay?"

"Yeah. Thanks for tonight . . . you know . . . " she told him, sliding out of the car.

Corinne got out of the cab and gave a little wave to Kyle as it pulled away. She wasn't ready to go inside, not yet, so she walked slowly around the side of the house to the backyard. She could hear Michael protesting about something from his bedroom above her and her father's tired, patient answer. Back in the hospital, her mother was waiting for morning. Corinne had seen the fear in her mother's eyes when she'd kissed her goodbye.

Why had she gone to the beach that afternoon? Why hadn't she seen how much her mom had needed her to be home with her? Two tears dripped off the end of her nose. She'd been a selfish *bitch,* more concerned with improving her tan and trying to get Jevon Harding's attention than in supporting her mother. Well, Corinne was done with trying to get Jevon to like her.

A window slid open behind her and Corinne turned around. Her father stood there, looking down from his bedroom. She gave a little wave.

"Don't stay out too long, Cori," he called. "The bugs are out."

"Sure," she said, but didn't go in. Instead she yanked some weeds out of a flowerbed. Then she pulled the finished blooms from some plants, watered the hanging baskets.

Pausing, she looked around at the garden. Her mom had been delighted with the work Corinne had done out here. It was something she had done *right* in a whole long list of things she hadn't.

Chapter 11

A pigeon strutted across the grass outside the classroom window. It was good-looking, as far as pigeons went; its feathers smooth and gray, its eyes beady and black. It walked as though it owned the stretch of grass, heck, owned the entire school grounds for that matter. It had been distracting Corinne for the past fifteen minutes with its cocky little walk. Not that it would take much this morning to distract her. While the teacher droned on and on about tense agreement and other incredibly useless crap, Corinne's eyes were on the pigeon and her head was in a hospital across town.

Her mother's surgery had been scheduled for eight. It was after ten now. How long would it take? Was she done? Would her mother wake up before Corinne got there? Her dad was coming to get her as soon as school was finished at noon. He had *promised* to be waiting right outside the front door.

Would her mother be in a lot of pain when she woke up from the anaesthetic? Or would they have her so doped up that she couldn't feel anything? Would she even recognize anyone? Would her mother look different? What would she look like, *there?* Would you be able to tell what they'd done?

"What part of speech is the word 'deliverance' in this sentence, Corinne?" the teacher asked.

Corinne turned from the window and stared blankly at the teacher.

"I don't know, a verb?" she guessed.

"Not exactly. Anyone else?" the teacher said with a shake of her head.

Corinne turned back to the window. The pigeon had flown off, leaving her alone with her thoughts. A bell rang and chairs pushed back as students got out of their seats for break. A now familiar tap on her back startled her and she jumped.

"Hey," Bree said. "You want to go outside for a bit?"

For the tiniest of seconds Corinne considered telling Bree what was going on with her mom but then she thought again. "No thanks."

"You sure? I've got cookies . . ." Bree grinned, waving a baggie in front of Corinne. "*Chocolate* cookies."

Corinne smiled but shook her head. "Not hungry," she explained. "Besides, I didn't get my chapters read last night." She held up the English novel.

"Whatever," Bree said and joined the rest of the class.

Corinne picked up her book and opened it to where she'd left off last time, but she could only stare at the words. Finally, just before the bell rang, she went to the girls' room and perched on a toilet, head in her arms. Why hadn't she just told Bree what was happening? In the few days they'd known each other they'd become friends. Bree called it like it was. She was funny and smart and didn't care what anyone else thought. *Pretty much the opposite of me,* Corinne admitted. Which was probably why she was drawn to her. But if Corinne had told her about her mom, Bree would have said how much it sucked and given her a sympathetic smile. And she really couldn't stand the sympathy, the "poor you" glances, the thoughts she knew were behind the sad smiles.

The bell rang but she stayed sitting. The other problem with telling people was that every time she did, it made it all so much more *real.* And there was just about as much reality in Corinne's life as she could stand at the moment.

She took a long time washing her hands and splashing her face with cold water, trying to cool the heat. She looked at the face in the mirror, wiping at the black smudges beneath her eyes.

The teacher looked up from the novel she was reading when Corinne came back into the room but said nothing. Corinne slipped into her seat and opened the book, pretending, at least, to be following along. Bree poked her in the shoulder but Corinne ignored her.

Corinne nearly tripped in her rush to get down the stairs and outside when the bell rang to dismiss class. As promised, there was her father, waiting for her beside the van.

"Dad." Corinne buried her face in his shirt. He smelled familiar and safe, although his arms shook as they held her. "How is she?" she asked, pulling away at last.

"She's having a bit of trouble breathing . . ."

"Why? What's wrong?" The knot, which had been throbbing dully all morning, burned inside Corinne's belly.

Her father pulled her close again. "It's just a reaction from the anaesthetic," he explained. "They're taking good care of her. Did you eat? Are you hungry?"

Corinne smiled a little to herself as she grabbed her pack from the sidewalk where she'd dropped it. That was her dad, quickly returning to safe, practical concerns.

"Maybe a little. Where's Michael?" she asked, glancing at her dad as he backed the van out of the parking spot. He hadn't shaved that morning and had pulled on yesterday's shorts. The T-shirt was clean, but it had a rip in one sleeve. His eyes were red-rimmed and she could see the shadow of his fear hiding there.

"Michael's with Torrie. He's happier there and it's one less person I have to worry about."

They stopped briefly and picked up some food and then headed to the hospital. Her mom was still in recovery, they were told. Corinne picked at her sandwich as she and her dad waited in her mom's room. Every time wheels rattled by on the floor they both looked up, only to sag a little when no one came through the door.

They finally brought Corinne's mom back to her room late that afternoon. She smiled weakly at them from the gurney. The orderlies transferred her to the hospital bed, moving her carefully, guiding the wires and machines to their position beside her. Corinne watched, keeping well away from the bed, but her dad was at his wife's side immediately.

"Oh thank God, Melinda," he moaned, sinking into the chair. He picked up her hand and held it to his lips.

Corinne turned away, embarrassed by such a naked display of need. Even turned towards the window she could hear his quiet sobs and her mother's whispered reassurances. She had never seen her father so frightened and it made her own fear that much worse. If he couldn't cope, how could she? What would happen to them if her mother didn't make it?

"Corinne?"

She turned around. Her mom reached out her hand and Corinne went to her side. She caught herself glancing at her mother's chest and looked away, embarrassed.

"It's okay, sweetie. You can look," her mom told her.

"There's nothing to see," Corinne said, then blushed. "I mean, there's just your hospital gown."

Her mom smiled a tiny smile. "I know that's what you meant but the other is true, too, isn't it? There isn't anything to see."

Corinne shook her head, tears pressing against the backs of her eyes. Her mother took her hand and held it. Her face was white, her eyes large in her face. There was no strength in the hand that held Corinne's.

"Does it hurt?" she asked.

"They're taking pretty good care of the pain right now. I feel a bit sick, that's all, from the anaesthetic."

She pulled gently on Corinne's hand, making her sit on the edge of the bed. Corinne sat gingerly, afraid of hurting her mom, afraid of dislodging anything.

The pressure was back behind her eyes and it took everything she had not to cry. Her mom looked so frail and tiny lying in the big white hospital bed. It was hard to look at her and believe she would be okay. Two fat drops rolled down Corinne's face and dripped off the end of her nose. Her mother reached up, wincing, and wiped them away.

Chapter 12

July 28

I've been home a week and am slowly regaining my strength. But my fear and anxiety about what comes next is draining what little strength I do have. I'm terrified that the cancer might have spread, terrified of the treatments that might lie ahead.

"Who is this Breanna, Cori?" her mom asked. "I haven't met her."

"No, but Dad did," Corinne explained, rolling her eyes at Bree over the tiny electric-blue phone. Bree grinned. "I promise she's not going to get me into any trouble."

"That's not what I asked."

"Then what's the problem?" Corinne demanded. The bus would come and go before this conversation was over if her mom didn't hurry up.

"I would have preferred to talk with you about this ahead of time, Corinne. Not over the phone."

"Well, I couldn't earlier. Bree just invited me now."

"You're only going to Metropolis?" her mom asked. "There and back, nowhere else?"

"Yes. And I'll be home by four," Corinne promised.

There was a pause on the other end of the line. Corinne rolled her eyes at Bree.

"Well . . ."

"Thanks, Mom. See you later!" Corinne snapped her cell phone shut and grinned at Bree. "We're set."

The bus arrived and the girls climbed in and found seats near the back. Bree immediately slid low and pressed her knees against the seat in front of her.

"Is your mother always like that?" she asked.

Corinne popped the last of her granola bar in her mouth. "Naw," she said once she'd swallowed. "It's just 'cause she's recovering from surgery, she's . . ." Corinne began. She could have kicked herself.

"Surgery?" Bree echoed, sitting up and staring at Corinne. "What'd she have surgery for? Is she okay?"

Staring at the graffiti-scarred seat in front of her, Corinne tried to decide what to tell Bree. Finally she let out a breath and spoke, keeping her gaze on the seat ahead of her — she didn't need to see that horrible pity look.

"My mom has cancer," she confessed.

"What kind?" Bree asked softly.

"Breast," Corinne said, flinching at the word.

"Geez, Cori, that *sucks*. Really." Then a second later Corinne heard her mutter, "Damn disease."

Corinne coughed, cleared her throat, and forced herself to look up. A fierce scowl sat across Bree's brow, her eyes dark with anger. Anger Corinne could deal with. Anger was familiar.

"I don't know what I could do," Bree said finally, the scowl fading. "But if you need anything, just call. I'm around. Oh, except for right after summer school when we're away, but otherwise I'm around."

"Sure, thanks." Corinne nodded. "So what are we shopping for anyway?" she asked a second later.

"My mom wants me to get something 'suitable' to wear to this big family thing we have to go to next month," Bree said.

"What's your mother's idea of suitable?"

"Pretty much anything that makes me want to gag."

* * *

They found a suitable dress in one of the first stores they went into and Bree disappeared into the changing room to try it on. Corinne flopped in the chair to wait. Finally Bree stepped out. She stood in front of Corinne in the calf-length silk cocktail dress, her striped hair standing out in loud contrast to the delicate colours of the fabric.

Corinne struggled to think of something positive to say, *anything*, but came up blank. "Uhhh . . ." she began.

Bree turned to look at herself in the mirror. She frowned as she studied her reflection, tilted her head to one side. "You know what this dress needs?" she said finally.

"No . . ." Did Bree actually think the dress worked for her?

"Army boots!"

They laughed so loud an older customer shot them a very dirty look and the salesperson rushed over to ask them to be quiet. Bree changed quickly and handed the dress back to the disapproving woman. When they got out of the store they collapsed into laughter again.

When she let herself into the house just after four that afternoon Corinne was still grinning. It had been the best afternoon. She couldn't remember the last time she'd laughed so hard and so often. Dropping her bag at the front door she went looking for her mom.

"I'm home!" she called out. "Mom? You here?"

She found her, finally, sitting on the couch in the family room, folding towels. "I'm home," she said, from the doorway.

"So I see," her mom said, grabbing another

towel from the basket by her feet. She winced as she sat up.

"I told you I'd take care of the laundry, Mom," Corinne said, crossing the room. She grabbed a towel, folded it, tossed it on the others and grabbed the next one.

"When, exactly?" Her mother demanded. "It's almost suppertime now, you still have homework." Corinne didn't answer. "Corinne, I really need to know I can count on —"

"I asked for *one* afternoon to do what I wanted," Corinne cried, throwing the purple towel down. "Just one! So could you just *back off?* Please?"

She swept all the towels into the basket and stormed from the room. In the laundry room Corinne removed the load of clothes from the dryer, threw the wet ones in, slammed the door shut, and set the timer. She folded the dry things and placed them in each person's basket then returned to the kitchen.

Rummaging through the freezer Corinne found a casserole and slipped it into the microwave to defrost. She was just about to make a salad when her mom came in.

"I'm sorry, Cori," her mother said, taking the tomatoes from Corinne's hands and wrapping her arms around her. "I'm . . ."

"I'm sorry too," Corinne whispered against her mother's shoulder. "I know you're stressed about . . . stuff."

Her mother laughed softly and pulled away. "That's one way to put it," she agreed.

Chapter 13

August 1

Getting away was just what I needed. I'm so
thankful Gayle is here with me. There are things
that only another survivor can understand. We
spend countless hours talking, healing . . .

Corinne rocked gently in the hammock, staring off
at the lake shimmering before her, one hand on the
book that lay open on her stomach. The novel had
to be read for Tuesday, when she returned to class,
but the warm Saturday afternoon air made her
want to nap, not study.

For the first time in a while she was completely
alone. Her mom had gone for a walk along the path
to the woods. There was nowhere Corinne had to
be and nothing (or almost nothing) she had to do.

She fell in and out of sleep, chasing bits of

dreams. At one point Corinne heard the creak of the little gate and knew her mom had returned from her brief walk. Another time she startled out of sleep when her novel slid off her stomach and thudded to the deck.

At last, reluctantly, she opened her eyes, yawning. She climbed out of the hammock and stretched out some of the stiffness. Her mother had fallen asleep in one of the loungers, her sun hat shifted to one side. Despite the heat of the afternoon, Corinne saw the goose bumps on her mom's arms. She found a blanket and spread it over her.

Since the surgery her mom tired so quickly and easily. Was this normal? *Ask Kyle.* But she didn't want to ask Kyle. Didn't want to make the whole miserable reality even more real by talking about it.

She hated the words that had become a part of their lives — biopsies, chemotherapy, white blood count, mastectomy. They were ugly.

But Kyle already knows the words. He's done this already.

Her mother's book slid off her lap and fell to the deck. Corinne leaned over to pick it up and saw that it was the journal. She dropped it on the lounger as though it had burned her fingers. She thought back to those first words she had read: "How can this have happened to me . . ." What Corinne wouldn't give now to go back to that time. The worries she'd had then seemed childish compared to what was going on in her life now. She climbed into the hammock so her back was to her mother and picked up her novel.

Gayle arrived an hour later with Kyle. She waved as she stepped onto the deck. "We're back and we've got snacks from the market. Anyone around here hungry?"

"As long as chocolate is involved," Corinne's mom said drowsily, "I'm always hungry."

She got up from the lounger and followed Gayle into the cabin.

Corinne climbed off the hammock, setting her book down reluctantly. It was actually a pretty good story — she was enjoying it. She smiled at Kyle and he gave her a half wave. They'd talked a bit on the ferry the day before about school, Kyle's sports. He was funny and honest, like Bree.

"You want to go for a walk or something?" he asked.

"Sure, I guess," Corinne said. "I'll let my mom know."

"Be sure to grab a couple of doughnuts," Kyle called after her.

Five minutes later, doughnuts in hand, they headed down the road together. Corinne was glad of the food because all of a sudden she didn't know what to say. This was the first time she'd been alone with Kyle since he'd held her the night before her mom's surgery.

"You been to Salt Spring before?" Kyle asked, licking the last of the sugar from his fingers.

"No, first time. You?"

"A couple of times. Before my parents separated we used to come sometimes, stay in a bed and breakfast," Kyle told her. Whistling under his breath, he leaned over and grabbed a stick, whacking the brush growing at the side of the road as they walked. Every once in a while, through the trees, Corinne caught a glimpse of the lake.

"Dad had a hard time convincing Mom to come," Corinne heard herself confessing. "All she wants to do these days is sleep. And then when they told her the cancer was in the lymph nodes too she locked herself in her room and cried." She flushed, wishing she hadn't said so much. But Kyle just nodded knowingly.

"That can be a hard thing to hear. My mom was pretty shaken too," he said, tossing his stick away. He stuffed his hands in the pockets of his shorts. "At the beginning," he went on, "just after she got her diagnosis, she got really depressed and that was hard for me and my dad. But then something changed and she was all positive and optimistic again."

"Really?" Corinne looked at him, amazed at how reassuring it was to hear his words, hear someone else echo her own experience.

"Hey," Kyle said suddenly, stopping on the road beside a small break in the brush. "There's a path here that leads down to the lake. Want to check it out?"

"I guess," Corinne said slowly, looking over

Kyle's shoulder. The narrow path disappeared almost immediately down a steep embankment. "You sure it's not too steep?"

"It's not too bad. There are lots of branches to hang on to," Kyle told her, already heading down.

Corinne raised her eyebrows but followed him cautiously. The first few feet were the worst, as he'd said, and then it was a fairly easy and quick climb down. At the bottom the path spread out onto a small beach, the lake shimmering beyond.

"How do you know about this?" Corinne asked, slipping out of her flip-flops.

"One time when Dad and I were out canoeing on the lake we pulled up here," he told her. "Did a bit of exploring . . ." His voice became muffled as he pulled his shirt over his head. "Discovered the path to the road. Cool, eh?"

"Sure," Corinne muttered, distracted by the sudden sight of Kyle's bare chest. *He's not nearly as muscular as Jevon. He's not like Jevon at all . . .*

She blushed. Was she really checking Kyle out?

"You want to go in?" Kyle asked, standing ankle deep in the water.

Corinne frowned. "I'm not wearing my bathing suit . . ."

Kyle grinned at her. "So? Who's going to see? Not me. I can't see anything without my glasses." Still she hesitated, hung up by the idea of wearing nothing but her bra and panties *outside*.

"The water feels awfully good," he teased,

walking deeper out into the lake.

The blood pounded in Corinne's ears as she made up her mind. Then, before she could talk herself out of it, she stripped off her shorts and T-shirt and ran for the water, squealing as the coolness hit her hot skin. Once in, she immediately forgot about what she was, or wasn't, wearing. She lay on her back and floated, staring up at the patch of blue bordered by the green tips of the evergreens. A peacefulness that she hadn't felt in a long time began to wash over her.

"Great, isn't it?" Kyle popped to the surface of the water beside her, his blonde hair plastered against his head. He'd left his glasses with his clothes and he squinted to see her.

"Yeah. I should get Mom down here. It might relax her."

"My mom sometimes went to the spa, you know. She always came back feeling calmer."

"This would be a cheaper way of relaxing, don't you think?" Corinne said, thinking of Romi and the day they had spent at the spa. She hadn't seen her friend since the beach party disaster.

"Probably," Kyle agreed with a chuckle. He paddled along beside her, blowing bubbles. "It helped though. I always hated that I could never do anything to make her feel better. When she was puking from the chemo or crying because she'd lost all her hair all I could do was stand around and watch. She said a hug helped but I know she was just saying that. I wanted to do something, you know? I mean, I was only ten. There wasn't a hell of a lot I *could* do, but I wanted to anyway."

"We used to fight all the time," Corinne said slowly. "About everything. I'd yell, she'd yell back then I'd yell some more. It was no big deal. Now if I argue with her, I feel guilty."

They swam to where several fallen trees lay partially submerged in the water, draped their arms over the log and rested.

"I just want things to go back to the way they used to be," Corinne said softly. "You know what I mean?"

"I know," Kyle assured her, his breath warm on her face.

Suddenly, Corinne leaned over and kissed him. She didn't know what came over her. Maybe it was because she felt utterly relaxed and comfortable, connected and safe for the first time in months. After the initial shock, she felt Kyle start to kiss her back. It only lasted a couple of seconds before she pulled away.

Kyle cleared his throat. "Maybe we should head back?" he suggested.

Corinne nodded.

Back on the beach they pulled on their clothes and then, with Kyle leading the way, they headed back up the narrow path. When they got to the road he fell into step beside Corinne but neither of them said anything.

Corinne was suddenly very self-conscious. She ran a hand through her wet hair. No doubt it was a bushy disaster. And God only knew what her face looked like with no makeup. To her surprise, she realized she didn't really care. And it didn't seem as though Kyle cared either. She glanced at him. Water dripped from his shorts, leaving a trail behind him as they walked. Tufts of hair stuck out from under his cap like little wings.

Did she really like him as more than a friend? Corinne stood still at the side of the quiet road as the answer came to her. *No.* She needed Kyle, but not as a boyfriend. The kiss had felt . . . wrong.

"About what happened, you know, back in the lake —" she began hesitantly.

Kyle jumped in quickly, as though he'd been waiting for an opening. "Yeah, about that . . . you're not mad, are you?" His hazel eyes searched Corinne's.

"No, of course not," she reassured him. A tiny frown creased her brow. What were the right words? She *couldn't* mess this up, it was too important. "I just, well . . . Maybe we could just be friends?"

"Oh, hey, yeah," Kyle said, sounding relieved. His face broke into a smile.

The tension broke and suddenly they were both laughing, the sound floating beyond them into the warm summer air.

* * *

The rest of the weekend slipped past quickly.

Corinne spent most of it with Kyle. They went for a long paddle in a rented canoe on Sunday afternoon and then drifted into the little shops spread around Ganges eating ice cream.

They talked about school, friends, his parents' divorce, their mothers' illnesses, themselves. And for the first time since her mother's breast cancer had become part of her life, Corinne felt like she was with someone who got it. No matter how sympathetic and kind Bree tried to be, she didn't understand, couldn't *know*. But Kyle knew this strange world Corinne and her family were now living in. Yet even when they weren't talking the silence was never awkward. She never felt a need to rush in and fill it.

Corinne was both relieved and disappointed when they drove onto the ferry Monday afternoon. She and Kyle found a spot to sit out on deck where they could watch the porpoises leap beside the big boat and the seagulls dive for food, screaming as they flew.

"Have a good time this weekend?" he asked, resting his head on his bent knees.

"The best," Corinne told him with a smile. "But I'll be glad to get home. Our neighbour was supposed to be looking after my garden but I have this fear that he's forgotten and everything's dried up and died."

Kyle laughed, his blonde hair blowing in the ocean breeze. "I'm sure it's fine. It's only been a few days."

"Well, I'll be happy when I can see for myself."

"I've never been much on gardening. You should see our yard at home. I can't even remember the last time someone weeded. I keep telling Mom to hire someone but she keeps saying she'll get to it."

"I didn't know I was even into it," Corinne admitted, tucking a strand of hair behind her ear. "It kind of started by accident, really. Mom bought all the stuff — the day we saw you at the mall, actually — and then she got the diagnosis."

Corinne paused, her throat tight. If she'd been with Romi, her friend would have put on her sympathetic face, patted Corinne's arm, shaken her head in pity, and changed the subject. But Kyle did none of those things. He waited for her to continue.

"Anyway," she went on finally, "the plants were all dying in their containers, and no one was doing anything with them, so I did. And it just kind of went from there."

"I did the same thing, Cori," Kyle confessed. "I figured it was because I was bad that Mom got sick so I became the most well-behaved kid you've ever seen. My room was spotless; I never argued with any adult, never left a single pea on my plate."

"How long did you manage to keep that up? I can't imagine Michael being that good."

Kyle laughed. "Mom finally convinced me her sickness had nothing to do with my being good."

"Well, if nothing else, the garden gives Mom

something nice to look at when she's resting," Corinne said with a shrug.

"I can't wait to see it. I heard your mom saying how beautiful it is."

Corinne smiled shyly at Kyle, thankful for his words, for his friendship.

"Mom starts her treatments this week," Corinne said a few minutes later. "Dad says she's terrified of what the chemo will do to her. I want to help, Kyle, but I don't know *how*."

"Offer to go with her to the appointment. Maybe holding her hand through that first scary one will be a help."

"I don't know if I could handle that." Corinne shuddered at the very thought.

"Your mother has to handle it."

The seagulls swooped and soared alongside the ferry, their cries carrying on the wind. A passenger beside Kyle and Corinne threw greasy French fries and pieces of bread crust at them, which they caught in midair and swallowed whole.

"I'll ask her."

Chapter 14

August 5

I can hardly hold the pen I'm shaking so hard. I feel as though I'm about to face the executioner! What will chemo do to me? How long until my hair falls out? I've already lost my breasts. How much more will I have to take?

The building housing the cancer clinic was nondescript but the small sign outside announcing its purpose set her mother trembling so hard Corinne and her father had to support her as they walked in. Corinne wasn't all that steady herself. What had she agreed to? She was not good with this kind of scene: the needles, hospital smells, sick people.

"I can't do this . . ." Her mom's eyes were large and frightened. Corinne squeezed her hand.

"You can. You will." Her dad's voice was firm as he led them through the front doors.

The waiting room was filled with people. Corinne struggled not to stare at the thin, pale faces, at the parade of hats, brightly coloured scarves, and turbans. She kept her focus on her mother as they found chairs and sat down to wait while her dad checked them in.

Eventually a nurse led them down a hall to the treatment room, but when she opened the door and they saw the others already sitting there, hooked up to all manner of machines, her mother shook her head and backed away.

"I can't go in there," she repeated over and over. She was suddenly physically stronger than she'd been in weeks.

"There's a private room we could put you in, if you'd prefer." The nurse seemed completely unsurprised by the reaction.

The private room didn't stop her mother's shaking, but at least they could be alone. The large easy chair was obviously meant for the patient but there were other places to sit. Corinne sat facing her mom and her father pulled a chair up on her right side, out of the way of the IV pole. They both held tightly to her mom's hands. Corinne felt that if they didn't keep hold of her, she might dash from the room and never be seen again.

"I've changed my mind," her mom whispered.

"This is going to help you, Melly," her father told her. "It's going to get rid of the cancer for good so we can get you well again."

Her dad kept talking in a low voice but Corinne stopped listening. She looked at him, wondering if he really believed what he was saying or if he was as scared as she was. There were a thousand other places Corinne would rather be, even her English class. At least at school Bree was there, making jokes, trying to get their teacher off topic, so completely herself with her zebra hair and ripped jeans.

Bree had decided to change her hair colour that afternoon. She had promised Corinne that tomorrow morning she'd be a new woman. She kept offering to give Corinne the make-over she had wanted all summer but Corinne wasn't brave enough to accept. Corinne blinked, forcing her attention back on what was happening in front of her.

"Melinda, are you ready to get started?"

Her mother's fingers gripped Corinne's so tightly the knuckles pressed painfully together as the nurse approached the little group. She held a heating pad, which she placed on Corinne's mom's arm. She explained everything as she did it, talking in a soft, low voice. The heating pad was to enlarge the veins in the arm. The IV held a saline solution that flushed the veins and then the chemo drip followed.

Corinne looked away as the nurse approached her mother's arm with the needle. She felt sick to her stomach but didn't let go of her mom's hand.

She heard Kyle's voice as they'd said goodbye Monday evening. "She'll be glad you're there with her, even if she doesn't say so."

Glancing at her trembling, pale mother, Corinne hoped he was right.

"I'm so glad you're both here with me." Her mother looked from her husband to Corinne, a weak smile on her face.

"Of course we're here, Melly."

"It's no big deal, Mom," Corinne told her with a bright smile.

As the chemo bag slowly emptied into her mother's arm, Corinne kept up a steady stream of chatter. She talked about the garden and how one nicotiana wasn't coping well where she'd put it and how a book had recommended a certain fertilizer. Her dad told some really lame jokes and gradually her mom sat back in her chair and let the tension run out of her. Corinne and her father exchanged relieved looks.

"And how's your class going? How much longer have you got?" her mother asked.

"Two weeks. The final is next Friday."

"That's gone quickly, hasn't it?"

It was hard to believe that summer school was almost done. But then, the summer was half over and what did she have to show for it? Corinne shook her head; she would not go down that road. Not now.

"Yeah," she said instead. She and Bree had already decided to get together to study for their final. Maybe go to the library or the beach . . .

"Did Corinne tell you about the B she got on her last quiz, Melly?" her dad asked.

"No. That's so great, Corinne! Good for you!" Her mother's voice was overly loud, her smile too bright.

"It's just a small part of our grade, Mom. Relax," Corinne muttered.

"Nonsense. It shows you're taking the class seriously, putting in effort," her mother insisted. "You've changed your attitude about school and studying and that makes all the difference."

"I'll just be glad when it's done," Corinne said, secretly pleased by their praise. She was glad they'd noticed her efforts despite everything else that was going on in their lives.

"We're finished?" Melinda asked as the IV was slipped from her hand later that afternoon. "I did it then. I really did it."

"Good for you, Mom," Corinne whispered. She'd done it too, she realized.

"Remember to take the anti-nausea pills every ten hours, and we'll see you in three weeks," the nurse told them as they walked out of the treatment room together.

Not even the reminder that they had to return could dampen her mom's spirits as they made their way to the car.

"Take me to the ocean, John. Let's get an ice cream and sit on the beach before we go home. I want to celebrate."

Chapter 15

August 10

My world has shrunk to the size of a bed or a couch. How is the treatment better than living with the cancer? This is no life. This is hell.

Corinne spooned pasta salad into her mouth, emptying the last of the containers of food friends had supplied after her mother's surgery. *Somebody needs to go shopping soon,* she thought, putting her dishes in the dishwasher. *Gee, I wonder who "somebody" might be?*

The doorbell rang. Corinne closed the dishwasher door and went to answer it before it could ring again and wake her mom. Although it would probably take more than the doorbell to wake her mother these days. She glanced at her, asleep on the couch, and then pulled the front door open.

Romi stood on the step, looking polished and confident with her black sunglasses and healthy glow. "You're home!" she cried. "I tried you on your cell but you didn't answer so I phoned here but no one answered. Didn't you get my message?"

"Mom told me you called," Corinne said, stepping out and pulling the door closed behind her. "But I'm at school till noon, Rom, remember? I have to turn my phone off at school."

"Oh, right. Well, it's been *ages* since I've seen you, and Peter is out with his grandparents tonight. I wondered if you wanted to come to a movie," Romi said.

Despite being an obvious second choice, Corinne ached to go out with Romi, to just walk down the front steps and keep going, but then she remembered her mother asleep on the couch, the little brother who would be walking in any second, the homework and studying she had to do.

"I'm sorry Romi, I can't tonight. Could we make it another day?" she asked.

"I guess . . ."

Corinne sat down on the step. "Want to sit down?" she said, patting the warm cement beside her. "I can talk for a few minutes now, if you want."

Romi glanced over Corinne's shoulder at the closed front door. She pulled off her sunglasses and frowned at Corinne. "Can't we go inside?" she asked.

"It's just that my mom's asleep on the couch and I don't want to wake her." *I don't want you to see her like this.*

"How's she doing?" Romi asked, lowering herself to the step.

"She had her first chemotherapy treatment last week and it's really knocked her out," Corinne explained. "She doesn't have any energy, just sleeps most of the time. It's been pretty rough on her."

"Yeah, I can imagine," Romi said, her brown eyes filled with sympathy.

Corinne looked away. This was why she had avoided returning Romi's calls, was reluctant to see her. *You can't imagine any of it,* she thought to herself. "Anyway," Corinne muttered out loud, "your toes look nice." She pointed at the tiny white daisies painted on Romi's big toes. Romi turned her foot from side to side and grinned.

"Aren't they adorable? I found this great little salon that does it. And it's really cheap," Romi told her, glancing surreptitiously at Corinne's bare feet.

Corinne followed her friend's glance. There wasn't much left of the pedicure she'd had at the start of the summer, just some scratched and faded "Crimson Sunset" nail polish. The smoothed skin had become rough and dry from wandering around barefoot and, to add to the overall glamour, she hadn't shaved her legs in days and was in desperate need of a haircut. Corinne grinned.

Romi looks as though she's just returned from a week at a resort, and I look like I've just returned from a month in the bush. And I don't really care.

"Sounds like a good find," she said.

"Yeah. Maybe we could go together next time," Romi suggested.

"Sure, maybe . . ."

"Couldn't we go up to your room?" Romi asked suddenly, shifting her position on the step.

Small waves of panic washed over Corinne. She quickly got to her feet. "I actually have a lot of studying to do," she blurted. "I should really get inside."

Romi stood up too, brushing the dirt from her pants. She studied Corinne for a second then slipped on her sunglasses. "Maybe we can go out next week to celebrate the end of your class?" she suggested.

"That sounds perfect, Romi, thanks," Corinne said. She was suddenly anxious for her friend to leave. She wanted to check on her mom and get back to her books.

When Romi got to the end of the driveway she turned and waved. Corinne waved back then went inside the silent house. If she was lucky she could get a couple of hours of study in before dinner. She felt like she was making progress but she'd be very glad when her exam had come and gone.

When Michael got home from Torrie's an hour later Corinne got him set in front of the TV with a bowl of tortilla chips then went back to her books.

But it felt like no time at all had passed before her little brother was pounding up the stairs.

"When's dinner, Cori? I'm hungry," Michael announced, flopping down on her bed. He kicked his feet against the desk chair.

"Quit it," Corinne snapped, smacking his knee. "I'm trying to study."

"But I'm hungry!"

"You just ate —"

"That was ages ago!"

"Then get something out of the fridge."

"There's nothing in the fridge!"

Corinne put her pen down and turned around. He was right about that. There wasn't much to eat. They'd finished the last of the frozen dinners the night before and no one had been to the grocery store for ages. She sighed and rubbed her temple. It was five-thirty. Their father would be home in half an hour, ravenous as usual. Michael looked at her hopefully. Corinne sighed again.

"Well come on then, brat," she said, standing. "Let's go see what we can find."

Ten minutes later Corinne and Michael stared at the collection of food piled on the counter. She'd found a package of ground beef in the back of the deep freeze, a jar of tomato sauce, some vegetables, and some pasta. It was kind of hot for a cooked meal but until they got some groceries it would have to do, she decided, throwing the meat in the microwave to defrost.

"While that's thawing," she said to Michael,

"you fill a big pot with water, okay? For the noodles. And I'll cut this onion and pepper to add to the sauce."

The microwave beeped just as she finished chopping the vegetables. She made a face as she unwrapped the bloody ground meat and slid it into the frying pan. It sizzled and spat fat at her as it hit the hot pan and she yelped as she jumped out of the way, swearing under breath. She turned down the heat and added the onions and peppers. She gave everything a stir then replaced the lid.

"Michael, you set the table," she called out as she headed for the backyard. "I'm just going outside to water."

The poor plants were limp in the heat of the afternoon and Corinne took her time, watering slowly and carefully, stopping to deadhead the flowers in the planters, pulling a weed or two. She breathed in deeply and smiled as a whiff of nicotiana came to her.

"CORINNE!"

Jolted out of her relaxed state, Corinne dropped the watering can and ran for the house. In the kitchen Michael was hopping from foot to foot, his face stricken as he pointed at the stove. The stench of burnt meat and onion filled the air. Corinne held her breath as she grabbed the frying pan.

"Why didn't you call me sooner?" she snapped at Michael as she set the pan down on a cold element. She lifted the lid and groaned. A

117

blackened mess stared up at her. There was no way they could eat that!

"I didn't know it was burning. You were cooking," Michael whined.

"I told you I was going outside! I told you to set the table!"

"It's not my fault you let the meat burn, Corinne!" Michael cried, tears in his eyes. "I want Mom!"

"What's going on in here?" their father asked, appearing in the doorway. Neither of them had heard the garage door go up.

"Corinne burned dinner and now she's blaming me!" Michael said quickly, shooting Corinne a dirty look.

"I can't stand it anymore!" Corinne cried, slamming the spoon down. Little bits of charred meat and vegetables splattered over her shirt, across the counter, and onto the floor. "I can't do it! It's not fair! I'm not the damn housekeeper!"

"We all have to pitch in, Corinne. No one likes this —" her father began.

"Bullshit! We're not all 'pitching in'," Corinne screamed, her face a mess of tears and snot and mascara. "You run away to work every day! And Michael disappears to Torrie's or some other friend's house. I'm here! Every day! Cleaning, cooking, taking care of Mom. ME! And it's not fair! I want a summer too!"

"THAT'S ENOUGH!" Her father's voice boomed through the kitchen, rattling the dishes in the cupboard, silencing Corinne. "None of us asked for this! Not me, not you, especially not your mother!"

Michael and Corinne stared at their father, their mouths hanging open, and then Michael began to cry and Corinne's own tears started up again. And then their father was crying too. He held open his arms and engulfed Corinne and her brother in a hug.

"I'm sorry, I'm so sorry. I shouldn't have yelled like that," he said into Corinne's hair. "I know it's hard. It isn't fair."

"I'm so afraid," Corinne whimpered. "What if Mom dies? What will we do without her?"

"I don't want Mom to die!" Michael cried, pulling back. But his father pulled him in tight again.

"Listen to me, both of you," he said gently. "I understand you're scared. But the doctor said Mom had a ninety-five percent chance of survival. We must stay positive. That's what Mom wants and needs. Okay?"

Corinne and Michael nodded and Michael sniffed. "What about dinner?" he asked. "I'm still hungry."

Corinne and her dad laughed and her dad swatted Michael on the backside. "We'll order something. Go choose a menu from the drawer."

Michael cheered and ran off.

"You okay, Cori?" her dad asked, standing.

Corinne nodded. She blew her nose and wiped

her eyes. "Yeah, I'm fine. Sorry about the mess," she said.

"Don't worry about it. We'll get it cleaned up. Put the pot in the sink with some water and baking soda. Go ahead and choose what you guys want to eat and order. I'm just going to check on your mother and change my clothes."

"Yeah, sure."

Corinne sat at the table and rested her chin on her hands. She looked around the kitchen and let out a long, slow sigh. She'd have to make a shopping list. And while she was at it, she'd better think about what they'd eat tomorrow night, and the night after that.

Chapter 16

August 25

I feel less than human now . . .

Leaning forward, Corinne loosened another dandelion from the ground, careful to pull up the whole root, and tossed it on her ever-growing pile. She sat back on her heels and brushed the loose soil from her gloves. It was amazing what a couple of days of rain did for the weed population, she thought, gazing around the flowerbeds. But even with the weeds the garden looked amazing. Everything was lush and full, the planters overflowing with colour and texture, the perennials tall and strongly scented. She smiled and then leaned in and grabbed another rogue weed.

The cell phone lying in the grass beside her

began to vibrate and sing. Pulling off her gloves Corinne flipped it open. "Hey, Kyle," she said. "I was just thinking of you, actually."

"Really?"

"Yeah, while I was pulling weeds . . ."

"You're not funny, Corinne," he told her. "Hey, did I leave my iPod at your place last night?"

"Haven't seen it, but I'll look around," Corinne promised.

The only person Corinne felt comfortable having over to the house was Kyle. There was no pity in his eyes when he looked at her mother, no "Oh poor you" pats on the arm. He made really bad jokes about the cancer and it was okay because he and his mom had been there. He didn't tiptoe around the illness or the treatments, but he didn't feel a need to ask about it constantly either. He talked about normal, everyday things. It was *restful* being with Kyle.

"You get your results today?" he asked.

"Nothing yet," she said. "Not that I'm in a huge hurry or anything."

"You know you did fine."

"Hey, Mom's finally feeling human again," she told him. "She actually had a bath and got dressed this morning." Corinne had done her best not to cheer when her mom had come down for breakfast. She hadn't eaten much but having her with them had been enough.

"That's good news. Maybe you could get out with Romi this week."

Corinne sighed. Why had she thought it was a good idea to talk to him about her strained friendship with Romi?

"Yeah, maybe."

"You have to try, Cori. You've been friends too long to just let it go now."

"I know that! God, Kyle! But that doesn't make it any easier, does it? We have nothing in common right now. Her life is all summer romance and mine is all Florence Nightingale."

"Well tell her that then," Kyle suggested.

"I don't want to talk about this anymore, Kyle!" Corinne snapped.

After their awkward visit on the front steps two weeks back, Corinne had realized just how far apart she and Romi had grown over the summer. It hadn't gotten any better in their few brief conversations since then. Romi was full of the fun she was having with Peter and, Corinne was guessing, the others in Peter's crowd. Her days were full of sunbathing at the beach, tubing on Cultus Lake, and camping at Golden Ears Park.

And, although Romi always asked how her mother was doing, Corinne kept the details to a minimum. Why would Romi want to hear about how tired her mother was all the time, how thin she was getting? It was easier to say she was doing "okay" and leave it at that.

"I'm sorry, Cori," Kyle said, breaking into Corinne's thoughts. "I didn't mean to push. Listen, I'm gonna be at my dad's this weekend but when I get back on Monday I'll give you a call and we'll go rollerblading on the seawall."

"Sure, sounds good."

They hung up and Corinne was just pulling on her gloves when she heard a strange sound coming from her mother's bedroom. Frowning, she looked up. Hearing it again she set her gloves down and went inside.

"Mom? Are you okay?" Corinne asked, peering around the door of the bedroom.

Her mom was sitting hunched before the dresser, a hairbrush in one hand, the other hand closed in a fist in her lap. Corinne crouched beside her mother, who opened her right hand without looking up. It was filled with short, grayish-brown hairs. The breeze from the bedroom fan caught some and lifted them into the air. They watched them float away.

Corinne's pulse quickened. For days now she'd been finding loose strands of hair around the house. The bald patches on the back of her mom's head grew bigger by the day but Corinne had said nothing, just looked away, not wanting to know.

"The doctor said this would happen," her mom whispered finally. "I hoped that maybe for me it would be different."

Her voice was so sad, so *forlorn* that Corinne's eyes burned. She put an arm around her mother's shoulders and hugged her. "But this tells us the stuff is working," she said. "Maybe you should just brush it out. Get it over with."

Her mother's face lost all colour and she laid the brush down on the dresser and met Corinne's eyes in the mirror. Then, with a shudder, she nodded. "You're right. Let's get this over with."

Corinne stood behind her mother in front of the mirror. It didn't take many strokes of the brush for all the hair to be gone, her mom sobbing quietly the whole time. When she was finished she laid the brush down on the dresser and turned around to look at Corinne.

Seeing her mother's head so fragile and unprotected was unnerving. Without her hair she didn't look like *her* mom anymore. She looked like a cancer patient now. There was no more hiding the truth from herself or anyone else.

Her mother was still watching her in the mirror and Corinne forced a smile. She ran her fingers across the skin of her mother's head. It was bumpy and smooth.

"You know, your head is a nice shape, Mom," she said.

"Please don't lie to me, Corinne." Her mom was shaking.

"I'm not lying. It is. See how your ears are nice and close to the sides, and how your forehead slopes? Your head is beautiful."

Her mom still looked doubtful but Corinne kept smiling. She leaned over and kissed the top of her mother's scalp. "Now. Where's that scarf Dad bought you?"

Corinne pawed through the drawers until she

found the magenta scarf her dad had picked out. She stood behind her again and carefully wrapped the scarf around her mother's bald head. She tied it snugly and tucked the ends away.

"Where'd you learn to do that?" her mother asked, touching the silk gently.

"Actually, Gayle showed me. She thought it might come in handy."

Her mother turned away from the mirror and took Corinne in her arms. "I hate that you had to learn how to wrap your mother's bald head, Corinne. But I'm thankful you did." She kissed Corinne's cheek then sighed. "I guess I'll have to get used to wearing a wig now. My grandmother always wore one. She always looked so well put together. Do you think I'll look well put together? Or will everyone know I'm a chemo head?"

"You'll just look beautiful," Corinne told her, struggling to believe her own words.

Chapter 17

september 4

Today was a good day. I feel almost.

Corinne walked in the door to find her mother sitting at the kitchen table, her journal and an empty plate in front of her.

Her mother stopped writing and looked up at her, smiling. "Did you get everything you needed for school?"

Corinne set her overflowing bags down on a kitchen chair. "Pretty much," she said. "I got a few things from Michael's list too. There was even a bit of money left over so I spent it —"

"On me, I hope," her mom interrupted with a smile.

Laughing, Corinne went to the fridge and grabbed the jug of iced tea. She poured herself a large glass, drinking it down in two swallows. Setting the glass on the counter she turned back to her mom. "You look good," she said.

"I feel stronger today."

"That's quicker than last time, isn't it?" Corinne asked. Her mom nodded.

"Well that's encouraging. I'm going to put this stuff away." Corinne picked up the bags of supplies.

"By the way, Romi called," her mom said, stopping Corinne.

Her pulse jumped as she waited for her mother's next words.

"She wondered when I might be feeling well enough for you two to go out."

There was a pause that Corinne didn't try to fill before her mom went on. "I got the sense that you've been hiding from her," her mom said, knitting her fingers together and resting them on the table. "Or maybe you're hiding me from Romi. It's embarrassing, how I look, isn't it?" she asked softly.

No matter how much healthier her mother looked compared to a week ago, she still looked like a cancer patient. The bright pink T-shirt and striped shorts she wore couldn't hide how thin she'd become and the white turban only made her translucent skin more obvious. She had penciled-in eyebrows and her lips were chapped.

But Corinne shook her head firmly. "I'm not embarrassed by how you look. I just can't stand the pity in people's eyes. Or the awkward silence when they try to figure out what to say. I've just been trying to protect you from that, that's all."

"I've been hiding from people too," her mom said. "But it's not doing me any good and it's not fair to my friends. But I'm ready now to let them help. Yes, people are awkward and pitying when they see me for the first time but they get used to it. Just like you did." Her mom raised her fake eyebrows and Corinne smiled sheepishly.

"We need our friends, Cori," she said softly.

"Yeah . . ." Corinne reluctantly agreed and, grabbing the bags of school supplies, escaped upstairs.

She dumped the bag of paper, notebooks, and pencils on her desk and dropped into the chair, thinking about what her mother had said. But before Corinne could convince herself to pick up the phone and call Romi, her cell went off.

"I'm back!" a familiar voice sang into the phone.

"Hey, Bree," Corinne said, grinning. "When'd you get home?"

"Saturday."

"How was it?"

"Awful."

Corinne grinned wider. "But at least you were well dressed," she reminded her friend.

"There's always that, I guess. So, enough with the small talk — did you pass?" Bree demanded.

"Did you?"

"Asked you first."

"Yeah, I passed."

"Grade?"

"B+," Corinne admitted proudly. The little slip of paper containing her final marks was tacked on a corner of her bulletin board. She'd never received such a good grade in *any* class before.

"Urgh," Bree groaned. "I only got a B. I knew I should have copied off you instead of the guy across the aisle."

"There's always next year."

"No bloody way! I'm done with that. We're gonna ace English 10. You did request Smithers, right? Third period?" Bree asked.

Corinne assured her she had.

"How's your mom doing?" Bree said, asking the question Corinne had known was coming.

"She's doing okay," she answered slowly. "She had her second chemo treatment about a week ago."

"Two down, three to go, right?"

"Yeah, something like that," Corinne agreed with a small laugh.

"And how are *you* doing?"

The question caught her off guard and for a second Corinne had to think about it. "I'm okay too," she said at last. "But I think for the first time in, like, ever, I'm ready for school to start."

They talked for a few more minutes, making plans to meet by the school sign the first day back. Corinne hung up and stared at the small blue phone lying in her palm. Finally she dialed Romi's number. She closed her eyes, inhaled slowly and let the breath go as she waited for her friend to answer.

"I'm sorry I haven't got back to you," she said quickly as soon as Romi answered.

"I thought maybe we weren't friends anymore or something."

"No, it's nothing like that . . ."

"So how come you didn't call me to go shopping?" Romi asked. "Your mom said you went with Kyle. Are you two going together or something?"

"We're just friends, Romi."

"Is that why you never call or want to get together anymore? Now you've got this new friend, this Kyle."

"Kyle has nothing to do with it."

"Then what is it?" Romi demanded. "Why won't you talk to me? I thought we were friends."

"We are friends, Romi, it's just hard, right now. You wouldn't understand." Her attention was caught by a snapshot of the two of them on her desk taken the previous summer at Kits beach, arms around each other's necks. Last summer — it seemed like so much more than a year had passed.

"No, I wouldn't understand because you never tell me anything, even when I ask!" Romi said, heatedly. "You told me your mom had cancer at the end of June and that was the last time you

131

shared *anything* with me about it."

Corinne felt her skin flush and squeezed her eyes tight against the sudden rush of tears. "You shut me out," Romi went on, mercilessly. "And then you tell me I wouldn't understand . . ."

"I don't want you to understand!" Corinne cried. "Don't you get that? I'm glad you don't know how horrible this all is, how *awful* this summer has been! My whole life is centred on my mom's cancer and her treatments. Around whether the chemo is actually working, whether she'll *survive!*" Tears streamed down her cheeks and her nose ran. She sniffed, pressing the heel of her hand into her eyes.

"I don't know much about what you and your mom are going through," Romi admitted. "But that doesn't mean I can't learn, Cori. I just want to be your friend."

Corinne wiped her nose on the back of her hand and cleared her throat. "I want that too, Rom," she admitted. "I'm not doing anything right now —"

"Hold on a sec, Cori. There's someone on the other line," Romi broke in and before Corinne could respond, she was gone. She was back a second later, giggling breathlessly into Corinne's ear.

"That was Peter," she explained needlessly. "A bunch of us are going to a movie."

"What —" Corinne began.

"Oh, some action thing that the guys want to see," Romi interrupted. "He'll be here in about ten minutes so I should get ready. I'm glad you called, Cori, but I really have to go now. I'm sorry."

Corinne pressed the end button and set her phone on the desk. Ever since her mom had told them she had breast cancer back in June, Corinne had feared the day she would lose her. She had never once thought that instead of grieving the loss of her mother, she'd be grieving the loss of her best friend.

Chapter 18

October 1

I've been feeling so well! But I'm worried that after my last treatment, I won't be protected anymore.

"Can I have more lasagna?" Michael asked, holding out his plate. His mouth was ringed with tomato sauce and he'd splattered some on his shirtfront.

"If you promise not to wear it this time," his mother told him.

"Who taught you to eat?" Corinne asked, watching him shovel the food into his mouth. She pretended to retch.

"I'm growing."

"Growing what? A tail? Horns?"

"Cut it out, you two," their father said mildly.

"Hey, Mom," Michael said between bites, "Torrie wants to know if I can stay over this weekend. His dad just bought him a new game for his Wii. Can I?"

"We'll see."

"Why do we have to see? Why can't you just say yes now? Huh? Why do I have to wait?"

"Because parents like making children wait for answers to their questions. You'll understand when you have kids someday."

"Not going to happen," Corinne said. "No one is ever going to want to be with him. Look at him!"

"Shut up, Corinne. At least I can get a date."

"You? A date? You're *ten!* You don't even know how to eat properly."

"I'm almost eleven!"

"Oh stop it, you two. You're making my head spin," their mother said at last, throwing Corinne a warning glance. She took another forkful of salad and chewed thoughtfully for a second. "You know, Gayle hasn't called in a few days to check up on me. I have some things she loaned me before . . . stuff she mentioned she needed back. Maybe I'll drive over there tonight and return them to her. Cori —"

"Is that a good idea, Mel?" Corinne's dad cut in, the usual note of worry in his voice. "Are you sure you're up to it?"

"I'm fine, John. I feel good, just a little tired. But I need to get out. Maybe Corinne would come with me?" she asked, turning to Corinne.

"Sure. I haven't talked to Kyle in a few days, actually. He never returned my last call."

They didn't say much on the short drive across town. Corinne sat looking out the window as the tree-lined streets slipped past them. It was almost completely dark. The leaves on the trees were growing more brilliant every day as it got colder and colder at night. Several nights had actually gotten cold enough for frost to appear on the grass.

"Thanks for coming with me," her mother said, breaking into Corinne's thoughts. "I'm feeling pretty good. By Christmas it will all be over. Then we can get started on putting our lives back in order."

Her mom squeezed Corinne's knee gently then left her hand sitting there. Corinne looked down at the rings on the fingers and the watch strapped to her wrist. Her mother was left-handed, the only one in the family. It had always bothered Corinne that her mother didn't wear her watch on the same arm as everyone else. As a child she would undo the strap and move it but her mother always put it back.

The Nortons' house looked empty when they pulled up in the driveway. There was no welcoming light over the front porch, no light in the front room. They walked slowly up the walkway side by side and stood on the step for a second staring at the door before Corinne finally rang the bell. It seemed like forever before a light came on and the door opened.

"Uh, hi," Kyle said, staring at them in surprise.

"Hi, Kyle. I'm sorry to just drop in, but I wanted to return some things your mother loaned me and I needed a bit of air. Is it a bad time?" Corinne's mom asked.

"I don't —" Kyle began just as Gayle appeared behind him.

"Melinda! Corinne!" she cried. "Come in, come in. What a pleasant surprise! Kyle, move out of the way so they can come in."

In no time their coats were off and they were settled on the sofa in the living room. Gayle chattered as she turned on the lights and hung up their coats then went into the kitchen to make tea.

"Doesn't it get dark early these days?" she called. "And so cold all of a sudden! The other day I went out in the morning in short sleeves and by noon I was freezing! Summer sure doesn't stick around, does it? Milk and sugar?" she asked, appearing in the doorway, a tea towel in her hands.

"And Corinne? How are you doing with your classes this year? Your mom told me how well you did in your summer class. It's amazing what you can accomplish when you try, isn't it?" Gayle asked, coming into the room with a full tray. She set it down on the coffee table in front of Corinne and her mother.

"Go ahead, go ahead! I was just lying down in

the other room, just to have a blink, as I always say, right Kyle? And wouldn't you know it, I fell asleep! I can't remember the last time I fell asleep at seven o'clock!"

She stopped suddenly and stared at Corinne and her mom, as though she'd forgotten who they were or why they would be in her living room at seven-thirty on a Thursday evening.

Kyle was still standing in the doorway, watching his mother's every move.

Corinne felt cold all of a sudden.

Kyle was watching Gayle the way her father watched her mother, as though she might suddenly just disappear.

"Why don't you and Kyle go into the other room so Gayle and I can have a bit of a visit?" Her mother nudged Corinne off the couch.

Reluctantly Kyle led Corinne upstairs to his room.

When they were alone Corinne turned around and faced him. "Something's happened, hasn't it?" she asked.

Kyle sank to the bed, his long legs spread out in front of him. He pushed his glasses up his nose and made a sound that was half moan, half sigh. "It's back," he said bluntly.

Corinne sat beside him. "When did you find out?"

"Last week. During her blood work." His voice was flat.

Corinne reached out and took Kyle's hand.

He stared at their joined fingers.

"Is there . . . what did they say?" Corinne had to force the words out of her mouth. She didn't want to know, didn't want to hear.

"It's spread all through her. There's nothing they can do. Nothing."

"Oh Kyle," Corinne whispered, her face ashen. "I'm so sorry." She wanted to reach out to him, to hold him, but hesitated, uncertain.

Kyle leaned forward on the bed and rested his elbows on his knees, his head in his hands. His breathing was deep, ragged; Corinne could see the shudder in his shoulders with every breath. Her own heart hurt and she blinked hard to keep back her tears.

Slowly she slid across the bed until she was right beside Kyle, their bodies making contact from knee to shoulder. She stretched an arm across his back.

"We always knew there was a chance, you know?" came his muffled voice. "Every six months she'd have the blood work and at first we'd get all stressed about it. But then we started taking the tests for granted when the results kept coming back fine. I forgot to worry. I let my guard down . . ."

His voice trailed away and for several minutes the only sound in the room was the ticking of Kyle's old-fashioned alarm clock. Corinne rubbed his back gently, at a loss for words.

"I don't know if it's really real yet, you know?"

Kyle said at last, sitting up. "It's like Mom told me and then nothing changed, even though everything has."

"How long . . . Did they say?"

"A while, I guess." Kyle said. "They weren't really sure. There's some treatments they want to try, but . . ." He shrugged.

"Your mom isn't sure if she wants to try? But what if they can help?" Corinne cried.

"They would only prolong the time she has left, Cori. They wouldn't change the outcome. She's still going to die."

Corinne shuddered. This was too close, too much! How could he just say that? If there was even the slightest chance . . . She wrenched her hand away and stood up, pacing the small room. Slowly her heart stopped racing and her thoughts slowed.

In the end, no matter how much she or Kyle or any of them paced or argued or lashed out, things would always come back to the same fact. She came to a stop by the window and leaned her forehead against the cool glass.

"I need honesty, Cori," Kyle said from the bed. "Mom, Dad, and I promised each other we'd be honest about everything. No sugarcoating, no fairy tale. No matter how hard or awful it gets, we agreed to be honest so we can help each other."

Corinne closed her eyes, thinking of how shut out she'd felt when her mom hadn't told her what was going on. When she turned around to face

Kyle again, the pain on his face was so raw, so *real* she was tempted to turn away again. Instead she slowly crossed the room and sat beside him again on the bed. She took his hands and looked into his eyes, glassy with unshed tears.

"I'll do whatever you need me to do, Kyle," she promised, her voice shaky.

"Thanks Cori. That means . . ." But then Kyle broke into great choking sobs.

Corinne held him close.

It is possible to cry yourself to sleep, Corinne realized when she opened her eyes later that night. The end-of-summer light had faded from the room and they were both bathed in shadow. Kyle was stretched out on the bed beside her, one arm thrown across her. She lay still, watching him, and eventually, exhausted by her own emotions, she drifted back to sleep herself.

* * *

The ride home the next morning was very quiet. Corinne stared out the window at a world transformed by frost. Shivering in the chilly car, she tucked her hands under her thighs, and thought about the night that had just passed.

Her mom and Gayle had talked long into the night. At some point, her mother had told her, they'd gone looking for their kids only to find them asleep on Kyle's bed, arms wrapped around each other. "We couldn't bear to wake you," her

141

mom had explained.

As soon as the car rolled into the garage, Corinne jumped out and ran for the backyard. She cringed as she looked over the flowerbeds. The frost had killed everything. All summer she had faithfully tended these flowers, watering, feeding, trimming, and cutting each one with love and dedication, and now, now it was for nothing. Corinne's throat tightened and she choked, suddenly unable to draw breath.

Sinking to her knees on the frozen ground she reached for a plant. The stalks and leaves were brown and mushy, the blossoms wilted and discoloured from the cold.

It took several good pulls to free the impatiens from the soil. Corinne nearly fell backwards when it finally popped out. She looked at the shreds in her hand and remembered the tiny, delicate bedding plant she'd put in the ground months before.

"It's amazing, isn't it?" her mother asked from behind her. "How much they grow in only a few months?"

Corinne put the dead plant on the ground beside her and pulled out another one. She heard her mother's knees crack as she knelt beside Corinne on the cold, damp grass. She held out a pair of gardening gloves and silently Corinne slipped them on.

"I've gotten a lot of pleasure from the garden this summer, Cori," her mom said quietly as they worked. "I hope you got as much pleasure working in it."

"I only did it for you, Mom." Corinne sat back on her heels and looked at her mother. "Because you couldn't."

Her mother smiled and touched Corinne's cheek with the back of a gloved hand. "I know it started out that way, but I don't think that's why you continued."

Corinne flushed. It was true, wasn't it? She'd found such a deep peace and satisfaction in working with the beautiful flowers and plants. Already she had begun planning next year's beds, reading the books, researching on the Internet.

Together they worked through each flowerbed, tossing the finished plants in a pile. Corinne pulled the last of the salvia from beneath the dogwood tree and tossed it onto the pile with the others, then rested her dirty gloves on her knees and stared at the sad-looking garden.

"How do you just watch someone you love die?" she whispered to the earth. Now that she didn't have the physical activity to keep her occupied, her chest hurt and her eyes stung. The cold air and her fear made her shiver. When her mom didn't answer right away, Corinne looked up to find her crying quietly. Slowly she crawled over beside her and they wrapped their arms around each other.

"I don't know, Corinne. I really don't."

Chapter 19

October 24

I've come to the end of this journal. And soon I'll
be onto the next stage in my treatments. There
are no promises with this disgusting disease. No
guarantees. We are all at its mercy. And yet,
even now, Gayle is remaining positive. How can I
be anything less myself? We must find the beauty
in each precious moment we are given.

Saturday morning Corinne slept late and woke to
the sound of the garage door rattling open. She
looked out her window and watched her dad move
the car out onto the driveway. A bucket and the
hose were sitting, waiting. She let the curtain drop
and went down the hall to the bathroom.

By the time she got to the kitchen her mother
was already folding laundry and Michael was in

front of the television, his favourite cartoon blaring. Corinne put some bread in the toaster oven and leaned against the counter.

"Good morning," her mother said, coming from the laundry room with a basket of clothes.

"Morning."

"Michael," their mom called, "take these clothes to your room and put them away." There was a grunt. "As soon as the show is over, Michael, please. And put them *in* the dresser, not on the dresser."

Corinne grinned as she pulled her toast out and quickly buttered it. "Where are you going this morning? You're all dressed up," she said. Her mother hadn't worn anything but sweats and jeans for weeks.

"Actually, we're going to the spa," her mom said, slipping into a seat across from Corinne.

Corinne looked up from her breakfast and frowned. "What do you mean, we?"

"I thought perhaps you might like to get your hair done."

Corinne self-consciously ran a hand over her hair. "Today?"

"Why not today? We're going to get facials and manicures too. And whatever else we feel like. And they'll feed us lunch!" Her mother clasped her hands together like a small child.

Corinne chewed slowly, eyeing her mother suspiciously. "Is something wrong? Is there something you have to tell me?"

"No! Corinne, no, there's nothing," her mom cried, crossing the room to hug her. She kissed her daughter's forehead, smoothed back her hair and kissed her again. "I just thought it would be nice to spend the day together spoiling ourselves. I think we both deserve it, don't you?"

Five months ago Corinne would have given anything to have what her mother was offering. Now it was hard to get excited about anything, hard to pull herself out of the dark cloud that had come down with Kyle's news.

She felt her mother's eyes on her, waiting for her answer. Forcing a smile, she nodded. "That sounds great, Mom," she heard herself say. "Just let me get dressed."

* * *

Monday morning the doorbell rang just as Corinne was shoving the last of her things into her backpack. She pulled the door open and grinned at Bree, waiting on the step.

"You ready?" her friend demanded.

"Yeah, yeah," Corinne muttered. "What's your hurry?"

"Always eager to begin another exciting day of learning, Cori!" Bree cried, rolling her eyes.

Corinne grinned. She'd resigned herself to walking to school mostly alone, figuring that Romi would walk with Peter so it had been a pleasant surprise when, on the first day of school,

Bree had showed up at the door.

"Morning, Bree," Corinne's mother said, coming down the stairs. She was dressed in yoga pants and a jacket and had wrapped her head in one of her colourful silk scarves.

"Hey, Melinda," Bree said. "Nice scarf."

"Thank you. Corinne picked it out for me."

Corinne leaned over and kissed her mom's cheek. "I'll see you this afternoon," she said. "You'll be here? No appointments?"

"I'll be here. Have a good day, sweetie. Good luck with that presentation," her mom said.

"Thanks, I'll need it."

Corinne slipped her backpack over her shoulders and hurried down the walk beside Bree, waving behind her as they went.

"So, what's with the new haircut?" Bree asked.

"Mom treated us both to a day at the spa," Corinne explained. "I even had a facial."

"Well, I'm not big on spas, but your hair looks great, Cori."

Corinne touched a hand to her hair. The stylist had thinned her heavy brown hair and cut it short so that it tucked behind her ears and left her neck exposed. And the whole thing was shot through with auburn highlights. She'd had a facial and her skin felt soft and fresh. Corinne grinned. She'd barely recognized the girl who stared back at her in the mirror that morning.

"You could be in one of those fashion magazines," Bree went on, studying Corinne seriously.

147

"Shut up, I could not," Corinne said, scowling.

"You're definitely competition for Jessica and her crowd now," Bree told her. "Although you're missing the attitude."

Corinne said nothing. Although she and Romi had managed to restore some of their closeness, their friendship was not the same — they had different priorities. Corinne spent as much time as she could with Kyle while Romi spent hers with Peter. And, although Corinne knew Romi would never be as superficial and snobbish as they were, Romi was friendly with Jessica and Jevon and the others now.

"What's your first period?" Bree asked, stepping through the school door Corinne held open for her.

"French. Then gym," Corinne said, making a face.

"My sympathies," Bree muttered. "I'll catch up with you later, 'kay? I need to use the can before first period."

Corinne found the books she needed for her first few classes, slipped her purse over her shoulder and snapped the lock back into place. She was mentally going over her morning when she turned around and nearly bumped into Jevon Harding.

"It's Corinne, right?" he asked.

"Yes." What did he want? Where were his buddies, waiting to laugh at her?

"You're a friend of Romi's, right?"

"Yes." Had she really thought this was the most gorgeous guy in school? There was nothing to him but a smile and big shoulders.

Jevon tapped the book on top of Corinne's pile. "You taking French with Abrams?" he asked.

"No, Toucette."

"Lucky. I had Abrams last year and she was lousy. I'm not taking French this year. Dropped it. It's not like I'm going to university or anything. You don't need French to drive a truck." Jevon shrugged as he grinned at her.

That smile! How she had longed for him to smile at her like that last year! Corinne nodded at him and started to move away.

"Romi says you're really into garage bands," Jevon continued.

"I guess," she said suspiciously.

"You hear there's going to be a festival next week?"

Corinne tried very hard not to laugh as she shook her head and mouthed the word no. She could not believe she was having this conversation with Jevon Harding.

"I really have to go, my friend is waiting for me," Corinne told him before he could go any further. She made sure she stayed long enough to see the look of complete surprise on his face before she hurried away.

Her thoughts swirled as she pushed through the crowds of students. Corinne passed a girls' room and slipped inside. She stood in front of the mirror and touched her short, streaked hair. Her brows were shaped and cleanly plucked, her makeup properly applied. She was not the same girl she had been last June. *That* girl had waited *forever* for Jevon Harding to notice her and would be doing cartwheels down the halls at this very second. That girl was long gone. But it had nothing to do with a day spent at the spa.

Epilogue

Corinne shut her eyes. Her throat was tight and tears stung her eyes. She could still feel Kyle's hand in her own. He'd stared so hard at the front of the church during the funeral, barely blinking, hardly breathing. The only sign of life was the sudden increases in pressure when he squeezed Corinne's fingers. Corinne opened her eyes and reread the entry that her mom had squeezed beneath the last line in her journal:

May 12

Gayle died today.

Corinne knew Kyle was seeing a grief counsellor. He'd been going for several months now. Did it help? Could anything help? They'd had so many months to prepare for Gayle's death, to talk about the things they needed to talk about and make the arrangements that needed to be made — like how Gayle wanted things to end and where Kyle would live afterwards.

In their endless talks through the fall and winter, Kyle had told Corinne about the discussions he and his mom had in the evenings. How much he was getting to know about his mother, about his own childhood.

When Corinne had looked at Kyle she was endlessly amazed at his strength and courage. Would she be able to do the same thing? How did a person not just crawl into bed and pull the covers up over their head?

Corinne closed the journal gently and set it on the bed. There were reasons all these things had happened. There are always reasons. She'd never have met Kyle and found the most important friendship of her life. She wouldn't have realized how important her family was to her, or become so close to her mom. She wouldn't have grown up.

There was a light tap on Corinne's bedroom door. "Come in," she called.

The door opened and her mom stood in the threshold. She had changed out of her formal clothes and into a pair of pale green capris and a white shirt. Her short hair was held back from her face with a wide green band and she was wearing white sandals. Her eyes were shadowed with grief and red-rimmed from crying, but she still looked young and healthy.

"You should get out of those clothes, Cori," she said, crossing the room.

"Yeah."

Her mother sat down beside her and leaned back on her hands.

"You're quite the writer," Corinne teased, tapping the journal with one fingertip.

"I enjoyed the writing, even if I didn't enjoy *what* I was writing," her mother confessed. "I think I'll get another one, keep going. Speaking of which, I have something for you." She handed Corinne a flat, wrapped package.

Corinne took it, confused. "What's this?" she asked as she peeled the daisy-covered paper away. Inside was a book, *"The Gardener's Notebook"* embossed on the cover. Corinne looked up at her mom, her eyes wide.

"For me? Why?" she asked, touching the beautiful lettering gently.

"Because you need a place to keep track of your thoughts. Not just about gardening, although I hope you'll do that, but also about life, relationships, whatever."

"It's beautiful Mom, thank you."

Corinne's mom took her hand, running her thumb gently across the palm.

"You made this past year bearable, Cori," her mom whispered, her voice catching. "You have become the most amazing young woman and I am so very grateful for you."

Corinne hugged her mom close and felt the

153

steady rhythm of their beating hearts. Gazing out the window over her mother's shoulder, she saw the blossoming trees, the spring flowers unfurling from the dark earth. And she smiled.

Acknowledgements

Coping with breast cancer is an extremely stressful and emotional experience for any family. One of the reasons we wrote this book was to help teen girls and their mothers understand and perhaps better appreciate each other's unique experiences when dealing with critical illness.

Special thanks to Ann, Cynthia, Joan, Kathleen, Linda, Margriet, and Norma, who were the first to give me feedback on this story many years ago; to Diane and Shelley, for sharing their expertise on writing for teens; and to Ellen, as always, for being my mentor, but more importantly, my friend. — S.D.

A very special thank you to Sandra for taking on this project and helping me to shape my story. I am so very grateful to the people who helped me travel my own breast cancer journey successfully: Dr. M. Glanzberg, Dr. G. McGregor, Dr. P. Clugston (in memoriam), Dr. K. Gelmon (my angel), Dr. D. Miller and the many nurses and technicians.

Thanks also to Jamie Brown at the BC Cancer Agency for answering our questions. — G.L.

Read more great teen fiction from SideStreets.

Ask for them at your local library, bookstore, or order them online at www.lorimer.ca.

Best Laid Plans
by Christine Hart

Robyn's family has always struggled to make enough money to survive. She desperately wants to go to university, but to make a better life for herself, she'll have to leave her pregnant younger sister behind.

ISBN: 978-1-55277-446-5 (paperback)

Ceiling Stars
by Sandra Diersch

Christine and Danelle have been friends forever. But lately Danelle's quirky moods have turned into wild and reckless acts. As the complex and dangerous truth behind her ups and downs becomes clear, the girls' friendship is put to the test.

ISBN: 1-55028-834-2 (paperback)

Strange Beauty
by Lori Weber

Beautiful girls get all the breaks, or so Penny thinks. Delving into her family's past, Penny discovers stories of former lives, and the startling connection between her grandmother and a strange old gypsy woman.

ISBN: 978-1-55028-941-1 (paperback)

Charged
by Carol Moreira

Craig is raising his younger brother while his mother is ruining their lives. Manda is dealing with parents on the verge of divorce. A moving story told from the point of view of two teens and their struggle to remain clean and true to each other while surrounded by their parents' world of infidelity, lies, and broken promises.

Tattoo Heaven
by Lori Weber

Jackie's dad has a new, much younger girlfriend, while her mom has started to devote all her attention to the sick girl next door. Torn between loyalties to both parents, yet struggling to find her place in their new lives, Jackie finds that the only thing keeping her from disappearing altogether is her butterfly tattoo.

Klepto
by Lori Weber

It's a big day for Kat's family — Hannah is coming home from a centre for troubled teens. But years of being dominated by her big sister's tantrums and wild escapades has left Kat dreading her return. The only place Kat feels in control is at the mall, where everything she wants is at her fingertips and no one is better at the art of stealing. As Hannah's return nears, Kat's shoplifting escalates into a full-blown addiction — with dangerous consequences.

LORIMER

Hell's Hotel
by Lesley Choyce
Tara thought she could handle anything, but now her life is falling apart. Maybe she's not so different from her friend Jenn, a homeless street teen, after all. Running away seems like the only option for Tara, until the night she spends in an abandoned building that kids on the street call Hell's Hotel.

Scarred
by Monique Polak
Becky feels numb, disconnected, and lonely. The only way she knows how to relieve the pressure she feels is to cut herself. But when Becky sees a gifted young friend heading down a similar path, she must somehow find the strength to deal with her own past so she can help her friend.

At Risk
by Jacqueline Guest
Tia is spending the summer working at an at-risk youth ranch. Spurred on by dreams of becoming a psychologist, she tries to bond with Sage, a street kid who has been given one last chance to get her life together. When money goes missing, it's up to Tia to find out who took it if she wants to clear Sage's name.

LORIMER

On the Game
by Monique Polak

There's nothing more exciting than first love — especially when the object of your affection showers you with gifts and attention. But when Yolande's new boyfriend, Etienne, asks her to go on a date with another guy, it becomes clear that his love comes at a terrible price.

Every Move
by Peter McPhee

Emily is living every girl's dream: she has two guys chasing her. Problem is, one of them doesn't know when to stop. At first Emily tries to ignore Michael's advances, telling him they're only friends, but as his letters and gifts escalate from flattering to frightening, she realized that his crush on her has become a full-blown obsession. The "dream" she's been living has become her worst nightmare.

Out of Time
by Peter McPhee

Three members of Eilean's tight-knit circle of friends have made a suicide pact. One carries through and another is very nearly successful. But when Eilean faces a race against time to find her third friend before it's too late, she finds an unexpected ally in Ron, the school bully who victimized the girls.

What people are saying about SideStreets

Praise for Sandra Diersch's *Ceiling Stars*
"[Teens] will love this realistic novel about
friendship, betrayal and romance. It is an
excellent tool to demonstrate the destructive
effects of bi-polar and depression."
— *The SouthWestern Ohio Young Adult
Materials Review Group*

Praise for Peter McPhee's *Runner*
"A page-turner with no happy ending,
this is a realistic picture of street life."
— *School Library Journal*

Praise for Monique Polak's *On the Game*
"Polak's cautionary work is hauntingly
convincing."
— *Montreal Review of Books*

Praise for Lesley Choyce's *Last Chance*
" . . . an outstanding read . . . This is a book
that's hard to put down."
— *Saint John Telegraph-Journal*